BEYOND
Me

the SEX ON THE BEACH series

BEYOND
Me

the SEX ON THE BEACH series

Jennifer Probst

The author acknowledges the copyrighted or trademarked status and trademark owners of the following wordmarks mentioned in this work of fiction: HGTV, Margaritaville, Mona Lisa, Pieta, David, Coke, Keds, Victoria's Secret, Coors Light, Alice in Wonderland, Sixteen Candles, The Walking Dead, Mission Impossible

Photo by: Getty Images (US), Inc
Edited by: Hollie Westring
Copy Edited by: Hollie Westring
Cover Designed by: Sarah Hansen at © OkayCreations.net
Interior Design and Formatting by: E.M. Tippetts Book Designs

Dear Reader,

Prepare yourself for Sex on the Beach, a trilogy featuring BETWEEN US (Jen McLaughlin), BEYOND ME (Jennifer Probst), and BEFORE YOU (Jenna Bennett). Three separate novellas. Three different authors. One literary world. Read them all, or just read one. It's up to you! No matter which route you choose, these standalone novellas are sure to satisfy your need for sizzling romance and an emotion packed story.

Happy Reading!
Jen, Jenna, and Jennifer

Praise for BEFORE YOU:

"The story felt fun, as Cassie enjoys the sunshine, and things develop and start to sizzle when she meets Ty. It kept me on the edge of my seat...and I was curling my toes at the romance." *–Bella, from A Prairie Girl Reads*

"A thrilling mystery mixed with romance and some much needed humor and wittiness, Before You is an enjoyable and gripping story." *–Stella, Ex Libris*

BEYOND ME

CAN FUN IN THE SUN TURN INTO LASTING LOVE?

Spring break in Key West with my besties was supposed to be casual fun. But I never expected to meet *him*. Sex and frolic? Yes! A relationship? No. But his hot blue eyes and confident manner drew me in. And when he let me see the man behind the mask, I fell hard, foolishly believing there could be a future for us. Of course, I never considered our relationship might be based on lies...or that his betrayal could rock my foundation and make me question everything I believed in...

OR WILL A LIFE BUILT ON LIES RUIN EVERYTHING?

The moment I saw her I knew I had to have her. She hooked me with her cool eyes and don't-touch-me attitude. I had it all—money, social status, and looks. I could get any girl I wanted...until her. When my friends challenged me with a bet to get her into bed by the end of the week, I couldn't pass it up. But sex wasn't supposed to turn into love. She wasn't supposed to change me, push me, and make me want more for myself. She wasn't supposed to wreck me in all ways. And now, if I can't turn my lies into truth, I just might lose her forever...

For two amazing women, writers, and now friends. Jen McLaughlin and Jenna Bennett, I never realized how much fun a project like this can be! You were truly a delight to work with. Thank you for helping me stretch my boundaries, dare to be different, and most of all, to rediscover my love for play in my projects.

Looking forward to drinking some Sex on the Beach with both of you in person soon!

Prologue

Saturday
Quinn

I watched the plane take off and wondered if I had made a big mistake.

The city of Chicago floated beneath me, and I was sent up into the clouds for a spring break I wasn't even sure I wanted. I sighed. So lame. Twenty-one years old and I was more comfortable working and studying than having fun.

"Don't even think about it," Mackenzie said. Her newly dyed chestnut, curly hair fell perfectly over her brow as she studied me. "If you keep it up, you'll have a breakdown. You need sun, sand, and sex."

I rolled my eyes. "Says you, because you're comfortable getting all of it, Miss Country Star. Or at least, most of it." That comment earned me a snort. "Me—I'm more used to rain and fog and sidewalks. This isn't gonna be like one of those spring break movies, right? Jocks slipping drugs into girls' drinks and taking photos of them to post on the Internet? Or sharks feeding on young bodies in a blood bath?"

Mackenzie groaned. "Way too much Lifetime TV, girlfriend. How about a tropical drink on a lounge chair, your toes in the sand, and some hot guy standing over you, bare chested and ready to serve all your needs?" Her eyebrows waggled up and down and I laughed.

"Maybe for you."

"Maybe for you, too, if you'd stop volunteering every spare second and recognized a man younger than seventy."

"Fine. I'll stop complaining since you were nice enough to finance the whole trip. At least I have my own room. I'm so sick of roommates and socks on the door."

My second best friend, Cassie, craned her neck and popped into the conversation. "I'm with Quinn. Finals are coming and I want my damn 4.0."

Mackenzie grabbed her magazine from the pouch in the seat in front and whipped out her iPod. "You two are hopeless. We are going to have fun on this trip, even if I have to force you. No books, no studying, no lameness. Got it?"

I grabbed her iPod. "You can't turn it on yet; it'll mess with the plane."

"That's just a superstition," Mac announced, trying to grab it back.

Cassie pulled the plug. "Quinn's right, I'm not crashing before I graduate."

Mackenzie groaned. "If it was a real problem, they'd take away our electronics at the gate. And how'd I get stuck in the middle seat, anyway? You're going to torture me all the way to Key West."

I met Cassie's gaze and giggled. Mac was the one with the money, fame, and outgoing personality. She was a country star by sixteen, thrust into the spotlight, and came to college to get an education and get lost. I hated country music—she's still mad at me for that—and had no idea who she was, even after she played me her top ten hit. Cassie was the studious one in our threesome, and probably one of the smartest, sweetest girls I knew. And me? Well, I was the worker bee. Save the world, one person at a time, I guess. I tried to get everything right so I didn't disappoint anyone, especially myself.

We'd met freshman year in English 101 and the moment we started chatting, something clicked. It was as if each of us brought something strong to the group, and I liked that.

I had lots of acquaintances at Chicago State, but Cassie and Mackenzie were true friends.

Cassie and Mac started arguing over the rules of turning on a Kindle, and I turned back to the window. Maybe this was a good thing for me. I was tired lately, and not up to my usual strict standards of achievement. A little sun and relaxation may jump-start me to finish the quarter strong, and getting prepared for my summer internship at the rehabilitation center. Maybe I'd even meet a cute boy I could flirt with. Even sleep with. Someone who could give me an orgasm. I was tired of reading about the experience in magazines and hearing about its greatness constantly in the dorm.

I settled my head back in the seat and tried not to hope for too much. After all, I was usually disappointed.

CHAPTER

Sunday
Quinn

A red Solo cup was thrust into my hands, and I automatically grabbed it. Foam spilled over the top and dripped on my flip-flops. I had never gotten into the taste of beer, and was hoping for one of those sweet cocktail drinks with the umbrella in it. Like Sex on the Beach. The girls had gotten me hooked, and I'd had my fair share since we landed. Of course, I wasn't at the hotel, and this was probably going to be the best I got. Unless I wanted hard liquor. I suppressed a shudder. I'd gotten drunk on rum once and threw up for hours. I still couldn't smell it without getting nauseous.

I forced myself to take a sip and maneuvered my way through the crowds, heading outside. The house was set up on a hill in a more rural part of the island, and reminded me of those mansions shown on HGTV. White with powder blue shutters, it was three stories and held an enormous deck that showcased the in-ground lagoon-type pool, tiki bar, and hot tub. Girls in tiny bikinis lounged on the side with their feet in. Some were on guys' shoulders doing chicken fights and pretending to be embarrassed when their tops slipped and they flashed the crowd. Of course, they had breasts, not like me, who was built with more of a slim frame and barely filled out a B cup. Boys stood in tight groups, drooling over beer, drooling over women, and drooling period.

Ah, crap. I shouldn't have come. The first day was perfect—we got off the plane, settled into our awesome rooms, and relaxed for the evening. The hotel was first class—Mackenzie only did top shelf—and the place boasted four restaurants, two pools, swim-up bars, a dance club, and the all-important room service. We swam and hung out the rest of the afternoon, then had dinner at the pool. That was the type of event I enjoyed—my best friends, beachy drinks, a stacked hamburger, and some laughs. But today they ditched me early, citing excuses about plans made already, so we arranged to meet at the local bar this evening. The first few hours were cool, but then I began to feel pretty pathetic alone in my one-piece suit while couples or groups swarmed around me. Then a girl with a bobbing red ponytail thrust a flyer in my hand and invited me to a party in one of the private villas on the island. Not that I was special. She handed them out to everyone in lounge chairs, chirping about how it was the party of the century and a tradition for Key West spring break.

I never went to places alone, with people I don't know. But I could only do so much sunbathing and pretending to read a hot romance on my Kindle. I was getting twitchy and bored. Water sports weren't my thing, so I figured, why not? Do something daring, Quinn. Go to a party where you're a stranger, and maybe meet a hot guy. Hook up, get laid, get happy.

Now, I wished I'd stayed put.

I sipped the lukewarm beer for something to do, and

found a spot near the balcony. Hooking my elbows over the top, I watched the show at the pool while music pounded out in grindy hip-hop rhythm to inspire abandon and nakedness. For one second, I wished I was the type of girl to climb in the pool, shake her ass, and enjoy a little feminine power. I always felt so out of place wherever I went, unless it revolved around work. Social scenes reminded me I wasn't flashy enough or bouncy enough or enough of anything.

Poor Quinn. At a cool party in Key West on spring break and complaining. My inner voice—who I termed my "inner bitch"—rose up and made me smother a giggle. I had gotten used to talking to myself back in the day and never got out of the habit. Sometimes I was my best company.

My gaze swept the pool deck to see if there was anyone I may know, or want to get to know, and then—*boom.*

There he was.

Mr. Perfect.

I blinked and tried to clear my vision. Trust me, I'm not one of the swoon-worthy girls who describes a guy like some male specimen. I've never been into the visual as much as enjoying a guy's sense of humor and conversation. Always thought I wasn't built that way. Even the first naked guy I saw on HBO didn't do it for me, and all my friends had gone on and on about his abs and ass and dick like they were dying to do him. Me—not so much.

But for the first time, I kind of lost my breath.

He wasn't movie-star handsome and didn't own rippling muscles or crazy tats or piercings. He leaned against the railing behind the bar, watching me, a tiny smirk resting on those full lips. As if I amused him by doing nothing. His hair was midnight black, rich against his tanned skin, and fell into perfect, tousled curls over his forehead. His eyes were a startling light blue, so pale they seemed to shimmer in his face with an odd light. I tried to break the gaze, but he wouldn't let me, just held my stare and refused to let go. As if the first one to look away lost.

I actually shivered under the hot sun. Something about that gleam of interest and laziness said he was trying to decide if he wanted to play the game. If he played, he'd bring it hard. This guy was no bumbling, inexperienced boy. Probably twenty-three, but his gaze said he'd seen things, done things, and would maybe like to do them with me.

He was bare chested, with plain navy-blue board shorts, and nicely built. Toned, but not overdone. His stomach rippled, and he stood with his feet slightly braced apart, as if he owned his space.

Whoa.

My heart fluttered in my chest, and suddenly my palms grew damp. I squeezed the railing tighter and tried to be cool. Ridiculous. He may be hot, but I don't think I even liked him. He was too confident, too used to girls falling over him and giving him what he wanted. I hated men like that—as if just by showing up they deserved more than anyone else. It was an entitlement thing, and since I'd had none of it, and had to work my way through every struggle in my life by myself, I didn't respect him.

He suddenly arched a brow, as if he read my thoughts and was even more amused. Usually, that would embarrass me enough to race inside to escape, but this time I did something that was quite unlike me. I gave him a tight smile, and deliberately turned my back on him.

There. Take that.

Way to go, Quinn. There goes your one opportunity to sleep with a guy who probably knows what he's doing.

Nah, not worth giving him another notch for his sexual belt. I did have my pride.

But not orgasms.

Please, shut up.

"I didn't even say anything. How can I shut up?"

Oh God, it was him. I knew it.

I dragged in a deep breath and turned around.

7

CHAPTER

James

The moment I saw her, my heart stopped.

I know it sounds like bullshit. That stuff doesn't happen. It's always glamorized in those pussy chick flicks. The music blares, their eyes meet, and you know they'll be fucking each other in the next half hour. Trust me, I've been with tons of girls, thought I was actually in love once but quickly got screwed—and not in a good way—and not once has my organ paused in my chest.

She was fucking gorgeous.

Not in the way I knew. I was so used to tons of makeup, tight, tanned bodies, and big tits. It's the way it is. I run in circles of society and money, and no matter how much I try to get out of it and despise the surface crap, I'm stuck. The few times I met a girl who seemed genuine, I found out later it was an act—a way to grab my attention and seem different.

But this girl rocked me. First off, she came alone, and seemed content to keep to herself. She watched from the edges of the party with a thoughtful, analyzing air that intrigued me. She emanated a quiet, confident presence that radiated around her, like she was a calm in the storm of chaos. She seemed completely removed from the laughter and antics in the pool and around the bar. Not necessarily above it all. Almost like she longed to join but had accepted she wasn't meant to belong. Her hair fell straight and silky past her shoulders and hid her face, like a screen that swayed back and forth in a game of peekaboo. It was a rich shade of brownish black that contrasted with her pale skin. Sort of like Snow White in modern day. When the curtain finally parted, I was fascinated by her face.

Large almond eyes, dark as sin, stared back at me. Her mouth looked swollen, as if she chewed on her lips as a nervous habit, but maybe they were natural. She owned stark features—high cheekbones, strong jaw, broad forehead. The one-piece bathing suit shouldn't have been sexy when surrounded by miniscule bikinis, but it was. Hell yeah it was. The simple black was demure in the front, but cut high on the thigh to emphasize gorgeous, non-ending legs. The thought of those calves gripping my hips as I thrust inside her made me hard. When she turned to the side, I realized the suit pretty much had no back, and the fabric stretched over her ass like a gift from the gods. I imagined cupping her, lifting her up so I could take her brutally against the wall, forcing moans from those lush lips, and biting them myself. Swirls of raw lust caught me off guard. She was unlike anyone I had ever seen, and my dick demanded to claim her.

Of course, this was when a few of my crew busted in on my lightbulb moment. "Fresh meat, James?" Rich pointed out from behind the bar. "You're eyeing her like you haven't eaten in a while."

"Anyone know who she is?" I asked, never taking my gaze from her.

"Nah, probably one of the spring breakers in for the week. Your parties are legendary here—and it's no secret pretty much everyone is invited." Rich studied her, then shrugged. "She's pretty. Nothing I'd be chasing though, especially with your options."

Adam jumped into the conversation, never one to be ignored. "Where's her group? Never saw girls come alone before."

"I think she did," I said.

"Looks snobby to me. Like she's too good for the others. Besides, she looks cold as ice. What the hell is she doing wearing a one-piece?"

"I think it's sexy as hell," I muttered. That was when I made my big mistake. Looking back, I wish I had kept my mouth shut and maybe things would've ended up differently.

My friends shared a knowing look. "You got it bad, bro," Adam commented. "But I'd bet not even you could tumble her."

Rich grinned. "Agreed. She's buttoned up so tight you'd need a crowbar to pry off that suit. Probably one of those control freak, studious types that doesn't know how to let loose." He gave a mock shudder. "No, thank you."

Suddenly, her gaze locked on mine. I sucked in my breath as recognition dawned on her face that I had been studying her. She stiffened but met me head-on, raising her chin slightly. I dove deep into a sensual heaven of swirling emotions I craved to figure out. She was so damn expressive, her thoughts flickering over that gorgeous face as she decided what to do next. I waited. Would she smile? Duck her head? Avert her gaze and pretend the connection never happened?

I raised my brow and upped the stakes.

One second. Two. She gave me a dismissing shake of the head and turned her back on me.

"Bro, she just dissed you!" The guys hooted, but I didn't care.

"It's a challenge." The gorgeous, sleek line of her spine

begged me to run my tongue down it until I stopped at the sweet spot. "Maybe I'm tired of the same type of women all the time."

Rich hooted with laughter. "Gorgeous, smart, sexy women who want to do anything for you? Yeah, cry me a fucking river. I still think you won't get anywhere with her."

Adam poked my shoulder. "When was the last time you got rejected? It's good for everyone once in a while."

"She won't reject me." The knowledge she was meant to be mine roared in my blood, but it was such a ridiculous feeling I decided to ignore it. She was probably playing games, and once I delved deeper, she'd be like all the rest. I was so sick of disappointment and emptiness beneath the surface. Not that I was any better. In fact, I was probably the worst culprit of all—an empty shell sucked dry of anything real for a long, long time.

"Care to make a bet?" Adam challenged.

"What type of bet?" I asked.

Rich drained his beer and looked triumphant. "Great idea. We bet you can't bed her within the week. We'll give you five days."

"Are we starring in some crap spring break movie?" The crudity of such a bet was disgusting and I waved my hand in the air, dismissing the idea. "I'm not into shit like that."

Rich cleared his throat. "Because you know you can't succeed?"

"Because it's a scummy thing to do. And none of your business."

"What if I put up something you've been wanting for a while?"

I turned my head. Rich seemed pretty confident I'd jump at the offer. I'd known him and Adam since high school. Our parents belonged to the same clubs in Florida and were all close friends. We'd grown up as trust fund babies, given pretty much free reign and anything we wanted. We sailed yachts together, travelled through Europe, and had been kicked out of too many schools. Seemed like a fucking great life until we got older and realized most of America didn't live that way. That there were things like real jobs and consequences and morality. My parents had none of that. They gave to charity because it made them look good, but turned their noses down at anyone who needed to scramble or get a bit dirty. When I hit about nineteen, I figured out they didn't like me much, and as long as I didn't embarrass their public image, they couldn't care less where I went or what I did. I did all the normal shit kids do to get attention—screwing up and trying to make their lives miserable because I couldn't please them. In return, they threatened to pull my money once in a while, and continued to freeze me out.

Once I reached drinking age, their attorney contacted me while they were travelling London. He had me sign on the dotted line, and all of my trust fund money was released, with a legal disclaimer that once it ran out, they weren't responsible for me. I got the big picture. I was on my own.

Of course, I'd always been on my own. I just hadn't realized it.

I jerked my attention back to my friend's proposal. "Trust me, Rich, I doubt you have anything I want that much."

He gave me a smug look. "How about Whit Bennigan?"

I cocked my head. I'd been heavy into art my whole life, but done nothing with it. I calmed my mind by going to museums, studying art history, and immersing myself in the visual world of professional artists. I had a room stocked with my paintings, but no one had seen them. No one really cared to. Whit Bennigan was one of the most famous painters in the south, and was making a name for himself to rival powerhouses. Using an edgy style with bold colors, he was a mix of old and new and was a master when it came to manipulating light. I'd read everything I could on the reclusive man.

"What about him?" I asked suspiciously.

"He's a close friend of my parents. He owes them a favor, and I could collect. What if I was able to score you a private lesson with him?"

I jerked back. "Are you fucking kidding me? One hour in the room with this guy could change my whole approach. There's no way you can bring that, Rich. You're full of shit."

"I'll bring it. You get Miss Snobby Pants into bed within five days, and I'll get you that lesson."

I turned and studied her. Back ramrod straight, dark hair spilling over her shoulders, looking at something I couldn't see out in the distance. I wanted her. Would've gone after her with or without a stupid bet, but at this point, what did I have to lose? I needed to have her, and a lesson with my mentor would be an added bonus. "What if I fail?"

The guys laughed. "We get your bike," they said in unison. Ah, shit.

My motorcycle was Harley, custom made, and sweet as sugar. It had an engine that revved like a thing of beauty, was badass black and chrome, and had every extra gadget I could squeeze on there. It had taken more than a year for them to make it to my specs, and it was my pride and joy.

"She still worth it?" Adam asked.

Yeah. She was. This was a bet I couldn't lose.

"Are we on?"

I turned to Rich, who'd asked the question. Glanced at the girl. And nodded. "Yeah. We're on."

Without hesitation, I pushed myself away from the bar and headed toward her.

CHAPTER *Three*

Quinn

His voice was rich and deep, and made my stomach flip when I thought of all the things he could whisper to me. Naughty things. I felt my cheeks go pink. Damn that inner voice. Now I looked like some crazed idiot.

"Umm, sorry, I thought you were someone else."

He made a point to look at the empty space around me. "Who?"

I frowned. "Someone," I said stubbornly. "Did you need something?"

He laughed. His eyes were even more spectacular close up, an aquamarine so clear and blue I felt like I could dive in and get lost. His hair was curly, and the color of yummy bittersweet chocolate. The strands fell over his forehead in a messy sexiness that looked made up. Yeah, he was way too perfect. Even his cheekbones and jaw were sharp and definitive, giving him an older, commanding look. Way out of my league. I self-consciously tucked a long strand of my hair behind my ear.

"You're the real welcoming sort, aren't you? What's your name?"

I paused for a beat. Just enough to get my point across—I was in charge of this conversation. My body disagreed as a strange heat pumped through my veins and itched under my skin. "Quinn. Quinn Harmon."

"Hello, Quinn Harmon. I'm James Hunt. It's nice to meet you."

I gazed at him with suspicion from under my lashes. "You too."

"Are you always this open and cheerful on break? I haven't seen you around—do you go to school in Florida?"

"No, I'm with two of my girlfriends for the week. We're from Chicago."

"Ah, the Windy City. I've been there a few times. State University?"

"Yes."

The conversation was painful, but he seemed delighted by my one-word answers. I wondered what his game was. Those full lips quirked slightly upward as if my crankiness made him happy. No wonder I couldn't get laid. I was more comfortable having a conversation regarding misplaced false teeth and what foods had to be avoided because they cause gas. Maybe working in an elderly home in my spare time wasn't such a great idea. Of course, soon I'd move into rehabilitation and be around alcohol and drug addicts. Probably not much better.

"Am I boring you already?"

I blinked. Did my blush deepen? "Oh, sorry."

He waited for more but I stopped. Stared at him. Our gazes locked and a weird, tight tension pulled between us. I forced down my impulse to take a step closer to soak up his body heat. He didn't smell of beer or smoke, but the clean scent of pool water and soap. "Are you enjoying the party?" he asked.

I nodded. "Yes."

"Did you bring your friends?"

"No, they kind of dumped me this afternoon at the Cove Suites, and this girl was handing out flyers, so I decided to check it out. Don't know who owns this place, though, do you?"

A wicked gleam sparked in those blue eyes. "Some rich kid probably."

"Must be nice," I muttered.

"The Cove Suites isn't cheap. It's one of the most exclusive hotels on the island."

"Oh, my friend Mackenzie treated us. I'm just a poor working student, but she insisted we stay there and get our own rooms. She's pretty generous."

"And your other friend?"

"Cassie? She's the serious type. Pretty brilliant, a bit more reserved."

"That leaves you? What do you bring to the group, Quinn?"

My throat closed up and I had no spit left. The way he said my name, his voice dropping low in a kind of caress, made me think of dark rooms and bedsheets and him naked. I hurriedly took a sip of warm beer and grimaced. "I'm the helper, I guess. Workaholic. All sorts of fun stuff."

He frowned, as if my remark didn't please him as much as my one-word answers had. "You don't like your drink," James stated. "Let me get you something else. What do you like?"

"Sex on the Beach," I blurted.

That grin was back. His teeth were very white and perfectly straight. He must have worn braces for years. Damn, even his teeth were sexy. "I like that too," he murmured.

Oh, wow, and now I had that image in my head—him and me entwined in the sand and his hands running all over my body, making me feel things I never had. I freaked out at my reaction, which kick-started my big mouth. "Just the drink."

"Too bad." He turned to go to the bar, but then I remembered I didn't know him at all, and the one rule I made my friends pinky swear on is to never, ever accept drinks from guys. Too many crappy stories on the Internet showing how a girl can be raped or manipulated.

My arm shot out. I wrapped my fingers around his bicep. His tight muscles jumped a bit under my touch, and his sun-warmed skin was slightly damp. Those eyes flared with a touch of lust. Wow, did he feel it too? "What is it?"

"I don't take drinks from strangers. I can get it myself."

He studied me for a while, as if trying to decide if I was smart or completely paranoid. "That's a good rule. Never know what jerks are out to drag you into bed."

I laughed nervously. "Well, I usually don't have that problem, especially around Mackenzie and Cassie."

"I disagree." His gaze focused on my lips, and I pressed them together to combat the jump in my belly. Nerves? Or was that arousal coming up from the deep dark caverns of my body to finally introduce herself?

"You haven't seen them," I pointed out.

"Don't need to. I've seen you."

Oh. Wow. I had nothing for that comeback. He was a master at this. "Does that usually work?"

He cocked his head. "What?"

"Lines. You're quite...smooth. Are you trying to get me into bed?"

The delight was back, dancing on his face. "Did it work? Will you go to bed with me?"

"No."

"Then there's your answer. Come with me to the bar for a drink, and I'll see if I can up my game for you."

He had the nerve to snag my fingers within his and lead me to the tiki bar. I planned to yank back from his touch, but he was so warm and strong, I decided to let it slide this once. Now I was beginning to like him, which was much worse. A player with a sense of humor was disastrous.

Unless...

I dove into the deep end and went for it. I'd have to see how the rest of the encounter went, but this was the reason I came for spring break. Sex. Sun. Sand. Relaxation. Maybe this was a sign.

James pounded his palm on the wood top. The guy playing bartender gave him a high five and winked at me. "Sex on the Beach, Rich."

"Niiice." Rich grabbed a glass and began working the bottles. "I finally get to do something creative. This is a beer crowd."

I watched him pour and mix with deft motions. Nothing funny got dropped in there, and when he slid it over, I took a sip and sighed. Perfect. My new fave drink. Mackenzie got me hooked on them the first night, and I had no desire to break my new habit. At least, not this week. "Thanks. I'm surprised there's a real bartender here and not just some kegs and wine set up."

Rich laughed. "Nah, we do things right, don't we, James?"

James gave him a weird look. "Guess this rich kid runs a top class show."

As if they had spoken in code, Rich nodded and moved to the end of the bar. I was suspicious, but then James swung his full attention toward me, and I blanked out the rest of my thoughts. I finally understood what happens when sheer lust overcomes your brain.

You become an idiot.

"So, Quinn Harmon, any big plans for your break?"

"No. Just hanging with my friends and resting by the pool. School and work have been a bit intense lately. How about you? What school do you go to?"

He waved a hand in the air like his story wasn't important. "Schools are all the same. What are you studying?"

"Counseling. I'm specializing in alcohol rehabilitation but also have experience with senior care. That's where one of my jobs is."

"Ah, that's what you mean about being the helper in the group. The field pays crap, you know."

I gave a little laugh. Like I didn't know that. "Yeah, that's why there are so many job openings. Money isn't everything. That's not my goal in life."

His stare intensified. I'd never had the feeling of a man's focus on me full power. Like he wanted to delve inside and explore me completely. It must be one of the ways he maneuvered himself into a girl's bed. Goosebumps broke out on my skin even though the sun was hot. "What is?" he asked softly.

I blinked. "Making a difference."

He pulled back, as if my answer surprised him. Maybe he thought I was some weird do-gooder nerd and not worthy of his coolness. Whatever. I wasn't about to change who I was just to score a hot guy. If so, I would've made that move in high school, but I was past such nonsense. "What do you do?" I challenged.

A shadow passed over his face. He stiffened, and I knew my question bothered him. Before I could delve further, he flashed a grin so blinding and white I got distracted. "Everything. I don't believe in being tied down to a job so I can die a slow death in some cubicle. Don't you want a broad range of experiences?"

I snorted. "Sure. I'd just need someone to finance it first."

"Get creative. Take a risk. You're young, live a little."

"You sound like my friend Mac. She's always telling me to loosen up and go for it." How many times have I longed to do something outside my comfort zone? I was always left behind on adventures to take care of my dad. To make sure I covered that extra shift and didn't let anyone down. To confirm I was able to save enough money to get through another semester of tuition. I was a twenty-one-year-old stress case. But I had accepted my fate a long time ago, and I despised whiners. I learned to take what I had and make it work for me. Cassie called me an old soul trapped in a hot young body. Many times I agreed. Except for the "hot" part.

Still, talking with James made those feelings stir again. Forget about rational decisions or how things would work out.

How sweet to grab the moment and let it take you wherever you wanted. Was it possible for me?

Damn, I wanted to find out.

As if he knew exactly what I was thinking, he leaned forward. His breath struck my lips, and I was transfixed by the shimmering heat in those baby blues. "Maybe we should run away together," he murmured. His hand reached out and he touched a lock of my hair. He rubbed it between his fingers as if he liked the texture and feel. "Do something crazy."

My heart beat and a tight ache throbbed between my legs. Wowza, it was like my body woke up after being Sleeping Beauty and was suddenly horny as hell. "Like what?" I whispered back.

"Ditch the party. Find somewhere private. See what happens."

Oh yeah, that was all code for sleeping together. Usually, I despised lines and playboy guys, but I'd never been so tempted before. It was spring break. A vacation from myself. There was no tomorrow or commitment or any of those issues to work out. Just fun. I heard Mackenzie's silent whoop in the background, telling me to go for it, and I opened my mouth to say—

I was suddenly pushed from behind. I jerked around. The pretty blonde from the pool laughed wildly. Her bikini top gaped loosely open to show half a bare breast. "Oops! Need anotha drink," she slurred, toppling onto the bar countertop, those impressive boobs distracting most of the guys gathered around. Her boyfriend or whatever was laughing, and ordered another shot of tequila for her. I frowned as I looked at her beautiful face, kind of twisted up, her green eyes halfway vacant. She was past drunk and into danger territory.

I knew I should mind my own business and get back to Mr. Steamy and his lovely offer. Instead, I grabbed the guy's arm. "No, she shouldn't have any more alcohol. She's had too much."

The guy laughed. "No worries, sweetheart. She's fine. She's

20

with me."

That made me even more nervous. Did she really know what was going on? He put his arm around her like she belonged to him, but she obviously had no idea what was happening, clutching the end of the glass counter like she hoped the spinning would stop. I spoke louder. "No, she's not fine. She could be on her way to alcohol poisoning. Look, let's get her up to a room so she can lay down for a bit."

The guy narrowed his gaze. The jolly laughter faded away. "Hey, James, who's the do-gooder? I got this covered. Cool?"

I glanced over. James studied the couple, his mind seeming to shift, and I knew he was going to let the whole thing go and try to get the focus back to us and the sex he was hoping to have with me. The girl knocked over my drink, and I watched the peachy liquid spill over while the girl went into hysterics, her hand loosely laying in the puddle. My temper reared. "Not cool," I answered. "Look, I'm not trying to be a bitch here, but she needs to lay off for a bit. Or she's gonna— "

A retching noise broke through the air. The girl let out the contents of her stomach over the bar while catcalls of "ugh" echoed loudly.

"Puke," I finished.

Her boyfriend or whatever stumbled back and made a face, suddenly not so hot to get her more tequila. Her face turned green, and she slumped toward the ground.

I jumped to catch her. "Get me some napkins," I ordered. James quickly grabbed a bunch and thrust them in my hands, and I cleaned her face as best I could. "Are there towels in the kitchen?"

James nodded. "I'll get you some clean ones and some water."

"Thanks." Hooking my arm under her pit, I held her up and guided her through the sliding glass doors and into the house. Funny, her boyfriend scurried away like the rat he was. Asshole.

"Don't feel so good," she muttered. She swayed on rubbery

legs, but I was well used to the drunken walk, usually with a man with triple the weight to move and take care of.

"You'll be okay. Let's get you to the bed." I eyed the stairs with trepidation, but finally found an unoccupied spare bedroom. I helped her sit on the edge of the mattress and she pressed a knuckle to her mouth. She didn't look so composed and perfect. She looked like a young girl, sick to her stomach, alone, and not sure what to do. "What's your name?"

"Tratchie."

"Tracey?"

She nodded. "Spinning. Stop."

"I'll try."

James came in the room with a bucket, towels, and a few bottles of water. "Thanks, I can take it from here."

He looked from me to Tracey, brows lowered in a frown. "Let me help. Do you think we need to call 911?"

I shook my head and began dumping water on one of the towels, smoothing it over her face and pushing back her hair. "I'd like to know how much she drank so far, but she hasn't passed out yet. She's thrown up already, so let's get some water in her system and see."

"Got it." I gently retied her bikini top so she was covered, and James uncapped the water and managed to get her to take some sips. She choked, but held it all down.

"So tired," she muttered, clutching the edges of the bed as it probably spun out of control.

"We'll let you sleep in a minute, Tracey. Can you tell me how much you drank? Do you remember?"

She closed her eyes, but I kept gently repeating my question over and over. "Tequila," she spit out. "Shots."

Ouch. Dad was a Scotch man, which was pretty nasty, but I'd seen what tequila had done to him one night, and he'd avoided it afterward. "How many shots? Three? Four?"

She held up a shaking hand with five fingers. I calculated her body weight, added another shot for good measure, and knew she'd be okay. Just a wicked hangover to end all others.

The fact I knew such research should've been depressing, but living with an alcoholic father and interning at the rehab had given me more knowledge than I ever wanted. "Okay, sweetie, let's get you to lie down."

We forced her take a few more sips. James helped me lay her down, and we covered her with the patchwork quilt from the bed. She moaned for a long time, but we kept watch, and she finally went to sleep. I left the bucket by the bed along with some water and faced James.

"Is she safe in here?" I asked. "I don't want that asshole to think he can take advantage of her."

His features hardened and he clenched his jaw. There was a bit of sexy stubble that gave him a rough edge I found interesting. "I won't let anyone in. Besides, he's moved on. He's not interested in passed-out women, trust me."

I crinkled my nose. "If he's a friend of yours, I'm not impressed." I know I come off snobby at times, but who people picked as their friends said a lot about their character. I was disappointed to think James hung out with the same crew.

"Not a friend. He just comes to the parties and knows me." He seemed to pick his words carefully. "We travel in the same circles."

"Asshole Central?"

He laughed and shook his head. "Hope not. Listen, I promise you she won't be bothered. Tracey tends to party a bit too hard and many of her friends are used to her overdoing it." He studied me hard. "You didn't even know her, but you were the only one who stepped in."

I shrugged. "Alcohol poisoning is serious stuff. I mean, I like to drink too and all, but I know my limits and try to have backup with my girlfriends if I'm gonna let myself go."

"Guess you don't go to many frat parties at school, huh?"

"Not really. " I eased open the door and we walked out, shutting it. Now he knew the extent of my lameness. I realized this wouldn't work. He wanted a party girl—fun, frolic, and a good fuck for the moment. No matter how hard I wanted to, I couldn't change who I was. I'd probably end up planning everything, just like I did the first time I got laid. By the time I had decided to lose my virginity, I was so stressed out about it going according to plan that I didn't even enjoy it. I pushed down the lingering disappointment at myself and forced a smile. "Well, it was nice chatting with you. See ya around."

I tried to walk away, but his hand shot out to grab my upper arm. "Did I say something wrong?" he demanded.

I blinked. "Umm, no, it's just that I'm sure you realized we're total opposites. You'll do better with one of those girls out there, I think." I jerked my head toward the giggling masses surrounding the pool and stream of gorgeous tanned bodies set up for display on lounge chairs. My one-piece suit and flip-flops screamed "amateur" and "stick-in-the-mud." I was so not spring break material. Mackenzie would be pissed I didn't wear the off-the-shoulder halter dress she picked out for me or the tiny red bikini she'd stuffed in my carry-on.

"Wow, I really failed this pickup. You're throwing me at other women within half an hour of meeting me. Is it my looks?"

I let out an impatient breath. "Of course not."

"My conversation?"

"No."

He dragged me a few steps in. The delicious scent of him rose to my nostrils, and his body heat could've burned me alive. My knees grew weak, just like one of those awful clichés I read about. "Then what happened to our plan to run off together and have an adventure?"

My lips parted. His gaze dropped to my mouth, and those blue eyes darkened with lust. Holy crap, he really wanted me. There was no denying the heat between us, and my body pulled so tight it seemed to almost hum with tension. He was going to kiss me, and I was going to let him. My breath strangled in my chest, and he bent closer. His full pouty lip held me motionless, and I reached an inch toward him to close the distance and—

"Yo, James, we're running out of beer in the back. You got

extra in the cooler? None are in the fridge."

James muttered a curse. I jumped away, the moment broken, and rubbed my hands over my arms. "Are you fucking kidding me? Why are you asking me—just go look."

The other guy glanced back and forth between us and grinned. "I interrupt something? Sorry, dude. There are some bedrooms open upstairs where you won't get bothered."

The creepiness of a house full of strangers having sex wasn't my thing. It was so public and casual. I always pictured a fling being a bit more romantic and secluded than screwing a stranger in the back room of some rich guy's house.

And why was he asking James about the beer? Were they co-hosting the party or something? My stomach suddenly twisted. "Who's the owner of this place?" I asked. "Is he even here?"

The guy widened his eyes and hooted with laughter. "Holy shit, is she messing with me?"

James clenched his teeth. "Dane. Enough." He grabbed my hand and tugged me down the hallway. "Ignore him, let's go somewhere to talk."

"That what you calling it these days, my man?" Dane continued. "What's the matter? She don't like the idea you're so rich you can pocket half of Key West without a second thought? You can always hang with me, sweets. I'm just the poor working class along with my buddy for the ride." Dane's tone took on a cruel tinge. "You know, the one who just refills the beer and doesn't bother him?"

I gasped. James was the owner? He was the rich kid who hosted the whole party? Anger cut through, long and deep, like a slice of a knife, and I turned on him. Of course, he'd been playing me. Having a bit of fun so he could laugh later, and entertain his buddies with his new conquest.

"You really want to play this card?" James asked him. I noticed his face completely changed, becoming cold and hard, and Dane realized he'd gone too far. James' eyes went flat and hard, like a shark, and he stood completely still, a strong power rushing from his figure. I knew two things at that moment. James was a lot more dangerous than I originally thought. He'd crush competition, get rid of anyone he didn't like, and play by his own rules. The rules of the rich.

The second thing I noticed was I couldn't keep my eyes off him. I was horribly turned on by that powerful streak.

I had to get the hell out of here.

Dane put his hand out. "Sorry, man, I'm a little drunk. Catch you later."

He disappeared and we were left alone. I shook as I tried to form all the words I wanted to fling at him. If there was one thing I hated more than anything else, it was lies. I'd grown up with them like a nest of snakes, ready to take a bite out of every piece of truth in my life. But I was on my own now, and got to choose my friends and my men. Screw him.

"I'm outta here."

"Wait!" He blocked my path and we faced each other like an old Western at noon. "Quinn, hold on a second. Let me explain."

"Why bother? I get it. You thought I was stupid and you'd have a bit of fun. Hope you enjoyed yourself. Now move."

He fisted his hands and muttered a curse. "Shit. I was going to tell you, I swear. I hadn't seen you before, and I just wanted you to know me as *me*—not the rich guy throwing the party."

The hurt was the worst. I'd actually begun to like him in the short time he spoke with me. But he didn't even trust me to think I'd be anything but interested in his stupid money or social standing. "Oh, well that explains things. Now I know you as *you*. And I'm leaving."

"*Fuck*. I made a mistake. I'm sorry. Just...stay."

"Do you even know half the people here? Are they even your friends, or are they a bunch of strangers you want to impress?"

His jaw clenched. "It's a tradition," he said tightly. "I open it up to anyone who wants to come, but I'm not trying to show off. Look, I was gonna tell you, but you seemed like you'd already prejudged the owner as an asshole."

He was right, but I didn't care. I felt betrayed, and I wanted to get as far away as possible. If Dane hadn't blurted it out, would James have told me? I had no idea if he could be trusted. How many times had I been disappointed by some male promising me things he never intended on doing?

Suddenly, I was depressed. Why did this always happen? Was there ever going to be a guy I fell for who had integrity? I pushed my hair back. "Forget it. I need to get back to the hotel and meet my friends, and you need to get back to yours. Keep an eye on Tracey. And thanks for the drink."

"Quinn—"

I ignored him, choosing to turn and walk out the other way instead of trying to get past him. I took the outside path past the pool, the bar, and down the gorgeous bluestone steps circling back down to the driveway. He didn't follow me.

I didn't think he would.

CHAPTER

Quinn

Captain Crow's was crowded, hot, and exactly what I needed to get my mind off this afternoon and *him*. By the time I got back to the hotel, grabbed something to eat, and got ready to meet the girls, I'd burned off some of my steam but not enough. This time, I was done. I would find one super hot guy I could fall in temporary lust with—morals be damned—and sleep with him. Have my frikkin' orgasm. And be happy.

"Whoa, that is not a happy face, darlin'." Mackenzie peeked from beneath her wide-brimmed sunhat that made her look more movie star than disguised ordinary college student. "But at least you dressed appropriately. 'Bout time."

Her gaze was all appreciation and approval. I'd fished out the sexy black halter dress and fuck-me heels hidden in the bottom of my suitcase. I put on a bit of lipstick and mascara, then curled my hair so it had a nice wave to the ends. Halfway tripping on the killer stilts I wasn't used to, I slid into the vacant bar stool they had saved for me.

Cassie slid over a drink, and waited till I sipped the familiar concoction of Sex on the Beach. Now if I could only get some on the beach instead of drinking it, I'd be set. "What's up? We leave you for one afternoon and you combust. I told you, Mackenzie. It's not a good idea to be split up."

Mackenzie rolled her eyes and did a lovely snort that I could never pull off without sounding like a pig. "If we stay together, no one gets laid. You guys would stay at the pool all day and never talk to anyone but each other."

My gaze met Cassie's and I sighed. Yep, that's exactly what we'd do and probably be happy. Maybe Mackenzie was right. Hell, she must be, since she already zeroed in on the guy with the tats and the lovely voice. If he was a musician to boot, she'd be toast. Goodbye technical virginity, as she liked to say. I always thought it was a hoot she was still a virgin, and she was the most outgoing, flirtiest in our crew.

Cassie sighed. "Yeah, I guess," she said glumly.

"Oh, for God's sakes, I'm not sentencing you to jail for the week! I swear, if both of you don't find someone by tomorrow, I'll find him myself."

"I thought I did," I muttered, burying my face in the drink.

"What? Who? When? Who?" Mackenzie demanded.

Anger still burned in my veins. I related the story briefly to my friends and my body relaxed a bit. Alcohol and girlfriends were the best antidotes to stupid men.

Cassie tapped her lip thoughtfully. "That's an odd thing to want to hide. You'd think he'd be bragging about his money and house to snag you. Right?"

I shifted uncomfortably on the seat. "Well, yeah, but he had plenty of opportunities to tell me the truth. I felt like an idiot."

"Did he defend himself?" Mackenzie asked.

"He said he wanted an opportunity to show me his real self, instead of me jumping to conclusions because he was rich."

As soon as the words popped out, I knew I was doomed. They knew honesty was my sticking point, and that I was a bit overzealous when it came to the quality. Cassie spoke gently. "Sweetie, maybe he was telling the truth. Maybe he just liked you and didn't want you to have expectations."

"Was he hot?" Mackenzie asked.

I shivered from the thought of his broad, muscular chest, and piercing blue eyes. "Yeah," I admitted. "Really hot."

"Explain."

"Curly dark hair, beautiful blue eyes. Tall. Lean. Perfect mouth."

Mackenzie grinned. "Like that guy over there?"

My head swung around and I came face to face with James. *Holy shit.*

He sat at the corner table with a few friends. A pitcher of beer served as the centerpiece, and they were all laughing at something, but he remained still, his gaze locked on mine just like he had at the party hours ago.

What was going on? Was he following me? Why was he here?

"I think that's definitely him," Cassie commented. "You're right, Quinn. He's smoking. And very into you from the looks of it."

My heart pounded and my palms felt slippery around the glass. A weird ache thrummed in my lower belly, as if I was hungry or thirsty or something, but I had an idea of what it was. He turned me on. Big time. This was not good. Right?

"What's he doing here?" I hissed, spinning back around.

Mackenzie looked delighted at my sudden interest in the male species. "Probably trying to find you. His friends look cute too. Maybe you can introduce Cassie to one of them."

"No!" Cassie and I blurted out.

Mac pouted and disappeared under her hat again. "Just trying to help."

"I can get my own man," Cassie said.

"Tock's clicking, girlfriend. Tick. Tock."

Cassie shot her an annoyed look, but a grin threatened her lips. "Okay, virgin girl."

That got Mackenzie to peek from under the brim. "Lowball shot. You're one too."

"You're right. Sorry."

"Can we refocus on my problem, please?" I said. "What should I do?"

"Well, you're not allowed to stay here with us and hide," Mackenzie announced. "Remember the rules. We don't meet anyone unless we split up. Now take your gorgeous ass outside to the tiki bar near the beach and find someone else if you don't want Mr. Blue Eyes for the week."

Damn. I hated to admit it, but I tended to suck at going up to men, and how could I find one at this bar if James was here? I certainly wasn't about to march up to his table after my departure this afternoon. Besides, maybe he was just hanging with his friends and it was a coincidence. Maybe he realized I was kind of lame and he'd rather be with one of those easier-type girls.

I drained the rest of my drink and stuck out my chin. "Fine. I'll try."

"That's my girl," Mackenzie said.

Cassie squeezed my hand. "Good luck. Be safe."

"You too. Call me if there are any problems. Meet Tuesday morning for breakfast?"

They agreed. I tentatively got myself back on the ground, tugged my dress down, and headed for the door. I refused to look toward the back, but felt a burning gaze stripping off the little dress, finding skin, and stroking with pleasure. I fought the goosebumps, raised my head high, and pretended I owned this outfit and heels.

Of course, being me, I stumbled over the first step, grabbed the door frame, and had to pull myself back up.

Such is my life.

The sun was hot and my heels clicked on the deck as I

got to the second bar. Groups clustered around, and Jimmy Buffett was crooning the pleasures of Margaritaville and sweet alcohol. Girls swayed and danced in their bikinis, and others were dressed up like me, but seemed a hell of a lot more comfortable and confident. I chewed on my lip, squeezed into an unknown group, and ordered another Sex on the Beach.

The bartender gave me a look of appreciation and winked. Hmm, not bad. But he was surrounded by a crazed crowd, and I could barely hear him ask what I wanted to drink over the noise. Not conducive to seduction. I gave him a nice tip, battled my way out, and tried looking approachable by the railing. I cocked my hip, screened my face to look approachable, and waited.

No one came.

Everyone seemed to be hanging with friends, overdrinking, and interested in their own conversations. Humiliation threatened, so I quickly gulped the rest of my drink and reconsidered the bartender.

"Hey, pretty girl, how are you?"

Relief flowed through my body as I turned to face my approacher. Kind of cute, average looking, blond hair, brown eyes. "Good, thanks." I searched for something witty to say. "Umm, having a good time?"

"Better now that I found you. I'm Trent."

Ouch. Kind of lame, but so was I. I smiled brilliantly. "Thanks. I'm Quinn."

"You want another drink?"

I lit up. "Yes, please. Sex on the Beach."

"The bartender's free over there," he pointed out. "I'll wait for you."

Disappointment flooded. He didn't even want to buy me a drink? Oh, well, maybe he didn't want to be taken advantage of. And I wouldn't have let him get it for me anyway, since that would've broken the rules of always keeping your drink in view. I inserted myself in the vacancy by the bar, got my third one of the night, and went back. He'd kept his promise and was

32

waiting for me. "So what brings you to Key West?" he asked.

"Spring break."

His eyes lit up. I guess he wasn't one for warming me up, because he stepped right into my space and began stroking my arm. "This is one hot outfit. I'm here on business for a few days. Got a luxury suite. You up for some privacy?"

His caress was kind of annoying. Probably thought he was being sexy, but he kept running his fingers up and down my arm like I was going to buckle with desire. And I didn't like the way he bragged about his suite, like I was some poor kid who'd be dazzled. Geez, was this it? No sparkling conversation or lead-up? My stomach remained quiet, and I admitted I felt nothing. I certainly wasn't going to sleep with someone who didn't excite me—what was the point?

I sighed and stepped away. "Not really," I said glumly.

His eyes widened with surprise, then turned ugly. "Whatever. Figured you'd be a tease." He walked off without a glance back, and that's when I knew I was done.

The hell with it. I'd face Mackenzie's wrath at breakfast Tuesday. My tan would make up for it. I was outta here.

I walked down Duval Street and decided to head to South Beach. It was just past sunset, so the party was still going strong in the bars and on the sidewalks. I'd walk on the beach, then hit the room for some TV. No one would know—I'd tell my friends I tried but only met a bunch of dickheads. Which was true.

The thought of James tortured me as I strolled. What was it about him that made everything in my body shiver? Now that I had some distance, I wasn't as pissed about his lie, but I'd never approach him again. Probably saving myself from a big mess. I hadn't even kissed him yet. What if I got weirdly attached, or I discovered he lied about more stuff? Tomorrow was another day. Maybe I'd try again with some new guy.

My heel dug into a small crater on the road and I almost went down. Enough. I had no one left to impress. I leaned over and unhooked one strap, wiggled it off my foot, and hopped up and down while I tried to get the second shoe off. The leather string got caught, I jumped again, and felt my ankle begin to twist.

Typical me.

My ass headed south and I prepared myself for a rough landing, when strong arms grabbed me from the back and straightened me out. I opened my mouth to thank my protector, but he wasn't done. Kneeling down, he reached for my ankle, and gently untangled my shoe. Then looked up.

"You!" I gasped.

His smile was brilliant. The sun flashed on those white teeth, and his ocean eyes gleamed with wickedness. "Yes, me. You didn't think I'd let you walk away that easy, did you?"

Slowly, he rose, trailing his fingers up my bare leg and spreading fire over my skin. Definitely not annoying. In fact, my thigh quivered as he paused at my knee, then reluctantly pulled away as he got to his feet.

I was a goner.

CHAPTER

James

The moment I saw her walk into the bar, I realized I'd do anything to fuck her.

Anything.

The guys were babbling about some shit—probably a girl—and the pitchers of beer were flowing free. I recognized her as soon as the door banged open and she made her way to the bar, sitting next to her girlfriends. She wobbled on those dangerous high heels, and I resisted the impulse to jump up and make sure she didn't fall. The protective instincts were strange, since females rarely aroused anything other than my desire to party and get laid. She slid on the bar stool and the skirt flipped up, revealing the long flash of pale white skin that stretched all the way to heaven.

My dick rocketed to life. I'd never been turned on so fast by anyone. The black fabric slashed across her breasts and left one shoulder bare. She had patches of light red on her skin, probably a burn. She was so fair she'd bake out here without enough sunscreen.

She'd done something to her hair, and the long silky length curled at the edges, giving her a bit of a messy look that was sexy as hell. Her friends seemed animated with conversation as they bent their heads together. One wore a wide-brimmed sunhat as if to hide from the crowd, but I could tell from the flash of her face she looked really familiar. The other one was also attractive, and seemed protective of Quinn, reaching out to squeeze her hand.

The beer pitchers emptied, and rounds of tequila began. One of my crew nudged my shoulder. "You buying, James?"

I nodded. Didn't I always?

I sat and studied her, enjoying being able to stare as long as I wanted. Suddenly, her friend jerked her head toward me, and Quinn spun around.

Like a sucker punch in the gut, my head reeled. Those sinfully dark eyes pinned me down and held me in her grip without mercy. My cock jumped, my jeans shrunk, and in those few seconds, I knew she was just as attracted to me.

Her mouth made a cute little O, then she turned around so quickly I was surprised she didn't get whiplash. Her friends spent awhile talking with her, but she never looked back at me. I waited. Bought another round. And watched as the woman of my wet dreams slid off the stool, adjusted her balance, and walked out with her head held high.

When she stumbled on the first stair, I laughed. Not at her clumsiness. At her magnificence. How could her discomfort in formal wear make me so happy?

Because she seems real, the voice whispered. And I haven't seen *real* for so long, I wasn't sure it existed anymore.

I waited it out a minute or two. Flagged down the server and told her to put the next two rounds on my card. "I'm heading out, guys."

Rich raised his glass. "Gonna try and tap the lottery

ticket?"

Irritation hit. What an asshole. I leaned in. "Listen up. I think it's best if you leave me and Quinn alone for the rest of the week. No interference. And keep your mouth shut about it. This is between me, you, and Adam. Got it?"

Rich sobered up and nodded. "Yeah, sorry, man. We settle up on Friday. No more screwing with you."

"Good. See ya later."

I headed out of Captain Crow's and found her talking to some shithead by the tiki bar. I hung back, intending to break up their little party if it got serious, but a few seconds later the guy walked away, and she looked disgusted. She grabbed the railing as she almost tripped down the steps, hit Duval Street, and began walking.

I followed. The swing of her hips and the curve of her ass were better than Monet's water lilies and sweeter than the *Mona Lisa*. I enjoyed the view, wondering if she was going back to her hotel, and that's when she stopped in the middle of the busy street and tried to rip off her shoes.

I was distracted by the sudden flash of her thighs as she leaned over. Her skirt flipped up, but too soon she jumped, toppled to the right, and poised for a bad fall. I swooped right in and caught her.

Sweet heaven. Her body felt perfect in my arms, full of softness and heat. I righted her, then knelt to finish removing her shoes. The shock and arousal in those inky eyes confirmed I was right. All I needed to do was play on her body's reaction, steamroll past her defenses, and get her into my bed.

Then keep her there.

"You!" she gasped.

I grinned. She was adorable. My hands tingled as I ran them up her leg and stroked the trembling flesh of her knee. I wanted to keep going higher until I dove into her sweet, hot pussy, but I kept my control. I'd already screwed up once. A second time would be deadly.

"Just your normal prince on horseback," I said easily.

If I kept it light and friendly, she may not give me a tongue blistering. At least, not the kind I wanted.

Her brows drew in a fierce frown, but she didn't move away. Her face flickered with an array of emotions before she seemed to settle. "Are you stalking me?" she finally asked.

"Now, that would make me creepy. I was just barhopping with the guys and noticed you. Were they your friends? Mackenzie and Cassie?"

"Yes."

"Did you leave because of me?"

She seemed surprised by my question. "No." Letting out an annoyed breath, she backtracked. "Okay, yes. I went to find someone else."

Hot jealousy chopped through me, but I kept cool. "Did you?"

"No. There are too many assholes in Key West."

I laughed. "Asshole Central, huh?"

Her lips tugged in a grin. I ached to press my mouth over hers and feel the lush curves. "Yeah, something like that. Why are you following me?"

"Because I've been thinking about you all day. Because I fucked up and wanted to apologize again. Because the thought of you finding some other guy to smile at and touch makes me want to go apeshit."

Her dark eyes widened. "That's a lot of reasons."

I chose my words carefully, knowing it was a turning point. "I'm not a liar. I want to spend some time with you so you can make your own decision and get to know me better. I'd like to walk with you, enjoy your company. May I?"

I wasn't used to asking women to spend some time with me. It was always the opposite, and suddenly I felt a flash of vulnerability. What if she said no and refused to talk to me again? I waited her out and realized how important it was that she agreed. How bad I wanted to spend more time with her—in bed and out.

"Okay."

I almost sagged with relief but managed to keep my man card. "Great. Where are we headed?"

"South Beach."

"Sounds like a plan." I fell in pace with her as we made our way down Duval. I'd been coming to Key West for years now, and I always loved the free spirit of the people. From the sunset parties, to the sailing and revelry, it was a place to get lost and yet somehow manage to be yourself at the same time. "I wanted to let you know Tracey is okay. I made sure she slept it off and took her home. No one bothered her."

"Good, I'm glad. I was worried."

She swung her hands back and forth like she was a bit nervous. I saw her teeth reach for her lips and confirmed she was a biter. Unfortunately, that just made me want to experiment with the other places on her body I could bite, so I firmly veered away from the image.

Down, boy.

"How old are you anyway?" she asked.

"Twenty-three. Please tell me you're of drinking age and I didn't serve you illegally."

She chuckled. I'd bet she'd never giggle. Another thing I liked. "I'm twenty-one. But I didn't see you carding at your door, so you could've been arrested."

I winced. She was right. I had gotten used to my parents greasing many officials' hands enough so I could do what I wanted without getting into trouble. The party was a yearly tradition, and I never got bothered. A sliver of shame cut through me. "Yeah, guilty as charged."

She swiveled her head and stared at me. Like she was trying to figure something out that didn't fit. "Did you graduate?"

I really hated these personal questions but figured I owed her. If I answered enough to keep her curiosity satisfied, I'd be able to move on to the good stuff. Like sex. Lots of sex. "Not really." I waited for her horror or for her to judge me as lacking. But she only waited me out, swinging her arms, like she was really interested in the story. "My parents threw me into Yale for law. I hated it. Made a fuss, got kicked out, and I went to Princeton. They thought maybe doctor. I thought not. Eventually, they gave up trying, and let me be. I decided to travel and find out what I wanted to do."

"I always wanted to travel," she said. "I think I'd pick Italy first."

"Why?"

"The food."

I laughed. "Yeah, the pasta and vino are killer. But the art is the best."

She sighed with longing. "Did you see the *Pieta*? Or *David*? I heard it's so massive it steals the air in the room."

I stared at her, my heart pounding. She spoke like she understood the beauty of art in a way most people never got. Shit, most of my friends just looked for the naked statues to compare their junk. I never got to have a decent intelligent conversation about something I loved. "That's a perfect description," I said. "Michelangelo takes cold marble and installs flesh and blood and emotion. The first time I saw *David* at the Academia, framed by the arched doorways, I cried. No one reaches for that type of mastery anymore. We're all too...lazy. Happy with being content or saying something's nice. There should be more."

She touched my arm and smiled. "How wonderful. You're an artist."

I jerked around. "No. I paint and study, but I'm not an artist."

She ignored me. "Yes, you are. It's like being anything—an actor or a writer. If you do it, you are. Getting published or scoring a movie deal is one of the goals, but it doesn't invalidate what you do."

An odd hunger clawed up from my gut. God, had anyone in my life ever simply accepted me for an artist? People clucked over my hobby, rolled their eyes, and generally made fun of the entire thing. Watch the little rich boy play at his paints and pretend he's important. It hurt so bad, I began hiding it undercover, disguising it as a hobby, but craving so much more. Ivy League schools blurred before me, when all I'd ever wanted was to go to art school. But that would be accepting what I really wanted.

That would mean I could fail. And then I'd have nothing left.

I fought a shudder and redirected the conversation. I'd given her enough. "How about you? Did you always know you wanted to go into social work?"

She shook her head. "No. But I'm good at it. Look, here's the beach."

Her comment was odd, and I knew there was more, but I let it go for now. No need for deep secrets to be revealed for either of us. I was familiar with the small beach at the southernmost tip of Key West. Wedged between a pier and hotel complex, it was a great spot to hit between bars and cool off. Some women were already topless, running off the families from the afternoon shift to be replaced by the nighttime crowd. The water was usually warm, and you could wade all the way out forever without ever going over your head.

Quinn grinned and stepped onto the sand, moving toward the shoreline. Her dress tugged in the breeze, exposing more of the delicious skin I couldn't wait to taste, and she dug her toes in and lifted her head up to the sky. Darkness bled into the shoreline and the moon peeked out. I watched her, happy and free in the moment, soaking up the simple pleasure.

"I guess you miss this in Chicago, huh?" I asked, brushing back the loose strands of hair from her face.

"This is pure heaven. I mean, don't get me wrong, I love living in a big city, I'm definitely a city type of girl. But the beach and sun make me feel a bit decadent."

Decadent. The word dropped from her lips like pure sex.

The wind plastered the flimsy fabric against her chest, and her nipples poked out from the halter top. Holy shit, she wasn't wearing a bra. I hadn't thought she was, but the evidence ruined me. I stared, trying not to, and imagined sucking on those points until they were red and wet and swollen for me. Music drifted from the restaurant/bar. I knew I should offer to get her a drink, go inside, chat, and be normal. But I wasn't feeling very chatty.

"James?"

"Huh?"

"You okay?"

"No." I'd never felt so alone in a public place. Like it was just Quinn and me and the moon overhead. I wrapped my fingers within hers and tugged.

She took the few steps forward. Her eyes assessed, as if she wondered if it was a good idea, but the flare of lust confirmed my decision. She wanted this; wanted me. And I was gonna give it to her.

"Do you know how fucking gorgeous you are?"

She bit at her lip and looked worried. "No, I'm not."

I laughed. Again, a first. I'd never had a woman completely reject a compliment. "Oh, yes, you are. Look at you. Your hot little body wrapped up in a little black dress. I want to strip it off, taste you everywhere, make you come. Make you scream." Her pupils dilated and she panted, holding still as I stroked her hair, her cheek, her naked shoulder. "But right now I'm just going to kiss you, Quinn."

I fisted my hands in her hair and held her still. Lowered my head.

"Okay," she whispered.

I smiled before I claimed her lips with mine.

CHAPTER

Quinn

*T*he heat seeped into my skin, my bones, my muscles, and began to burn me alive. Warm water swirled around my ankles, the sand was firm and damp under my feet, and he trapped my head so I couldn't move. Not that I wanted to. The strength and bit of domination gave me a dark thrill. No man had ever wanted to kiss me this bad. And I had never wanted to be kissed like it was as important as my next breath.

His lips covered mine completely, as if savoring me, like an appetizer before the holiday dinner. I rested my hands on his shoulders for balance and enjoyed the sensation. Slow, sweet, exploratory. His tongue traced the seam of my lips for entrance, and I allowed him full access.

His tongue plunged into my mouth and the world exploded.

I gasped at his delicious taste, a slight sting of alcohol and a raw hunger that devoured me alive. He moved his hands from my hair to cup my face, his tongue dipping in and out of my mouth as if gathering honey, taking me over completely until the ground shifted and I could only cling to him, wanting more. He nipped my bottom lip, then sucked. The sharp pain gave way to heat that flicked my skin, tightened my nipples, and made me crave something really, really bad.

"So good," he groaned. "Like candy." His deft fingers stroked under my chin, down my neck, and across the swell of my breasts. I twisted in his grasp and tried to get closer, but he only laughed and kissed me deeper, while his fingers touched my nipples.

I forgot we were on a public beach and almost begged for him to pull down my dress. I felt achy all over, so I pressed against him and those hard muscles surrounded me with a power I wanted everywhere—over me, under me, in me. "Oh God, I want—"

"Yes, baby, me too. I want to touch you, kiss you, fuck you." His dirty words made me gasp, and he swallowed the sound, moving his fingers from my breasts to my rear. He cupped my ass and pulled me hard against him. His erection seemed massive behind the ridge of his jeans. I imagined him slipping between my thighs and I moaned again, sinking into an animal state where I didn't care about anything except slaking the ache.

"James. Please."

He breathed heavily, and when he finally lifted his head, those aquamarine eyes sucked me in, foggy with lust and naked want. I went to reach for him again, but the sound of laughter close by made me stiffen as reality leaked in. Holy shit, I was on a public beach with people everywhere! This was not like me at all; I was an extremely private person. The thought of strangers watching me practically climb on him with my dress exposing my girly parts freaked me out. Shaking, I tried to pull back, but he realized I was upset and tightened his hold. Tucking my head under his chin, he pressed a kiss into my hair, gently caressing my back.

"I can't believe I did that," I muttered against his chest. His T-shirt was soft and smelled like Snuggle dryer sheets.

"Shh, my fault. I got crazy. I want you so bad, Quinn. I'd love for you to come back to my house so we can finish what we started, but I think it's too soon. I screwed up once, I'm not going to do it again."

His words both comforted and disappointed. I halfway wanted him to haul me in his arms, drag me to the hotel, and give me no choice. My brain began to uncloud, and I realized he was right. I loved the idea of having a quick night, but honestly, when it came to ripping off my clothes and actually having sex, I kind of liked to know a guy better.

His control confirmed another layer of my trust. Did he do it on purpose? And if so, did it really matter? We both wanted each other. We had the week stretched ahead of us, and my goal was to let go a bit and live. What was I fighting so hard to protect?

I relaxed in his arms and enjoyed being wrapped up tight. Safe. Weird, I was always the one in charge and taking care of people. Had anyone ever made *me* feel protected? "Thank you," I finally said. "Things got a bit out of control."

His chest rumbled with laughter. He pressed a kiss to the top of my head. "I like the idea of getting you so hot you forget we're in public," he teased. He pulled back and tipped up my chin, forcing me to meet his gaze. "But don't get me wrong, Quinn. I'm not going to be able to wait much longer. You make me a little crazy."

I smiled. "Crazy is good, right?"

He kissed me again, slow and sweet, with the moonlight streaming over us. "Yeah," he said softly. "Come sailing with me tomorrow."

I tried to think if I'd made any plans. I had none. Mackenzie had been insistent we separate until our breakfast meeting on Tuesday. It was all in her master plan to make sure we came back with two less virgins and one who finally orgasmed. So embarrassing. "That sounds like fun."

"Good. Come to the marina at eleven."

"You have a boat?"

He grinned. "Sure. My parents taught me all the necessary skills for success in life. Tennis. Sailing. Keeping a stiff upper lip. And preserving appearances at all costs." Darkness flashed and stole some of the humor in his eyes, but then he was kissing me again and I didn't care. He groaned and finally stepped away. "You're addicting. I can't keep my hands off you."

Pleasure tingled in my veins. I wasn't the type to inspire men to want to rip off my clothes, they usually would rather discuss a situation or be friends. I was glad the dark hid my pink cheeks so I didn't look like a virginal idiot. "Fishing?" I asked.

"Do you want to?"

I shook my head. "No, I feel too bad for the fish."

"Then we'll let the water take us wherever we want."

The image of being with him alone on a boat in Key West made excitement unfurl in my belly. Oh yeah. I'd be sleeping with him tomorrow if everything went okay. But did I trust him to be out on the water without anyone else?

Yes. Hell yes.

"I'd like that," I said.

"Good. Let's exchange numbers." We input our respective contact information, then he grabbed my hand and tugged me away from the water. "I'll walk you to the hotel."

The stroll back was leisurely and quiet. It was nice to relax and not worry about conversation, and he seemed to enjoy it just as much. He swung my hand was we walked, commenting here and there on some areas of attractions I may want to see during the week, and when we reached the hotel lobby, gave me a gentle kiss on the lips.

But his eyes blazed a promise I wanted him to keep.

"Night, Quinn."

"Night, James."

He waited until I went inside. My legs trembled as I got

to my room. I barely got through the door before my phone rang. I jumped—no one usually called me when texting was so much easier. I glanced down, saw Cassie's name, and almost panicked.

"Are you okay?" I asked as soon as I heard her voice.

"Fine. Are you?"

Weird question. "Sure. Why?"

A pause. "Just checking. I met this guy—" She trailed off. "He convinced me to call to make sure you got home in one piece."

My body slumped in relief. Why did I always have to be the paranoid one in the group? I couldn't help the little chuckle that escaped. "Oh." I figured he was right there and she couldn't talk, but I couldn't help teasing her a bit. "This guy sounds pretty special if he's checking up on your friends."

"Shut up." I heard the grin in her voice. "Are you at the hotel?"

"Yeah, just walked in. Where's Mackenzie?"

"Found her hot musician with tattoos. Dumped me pretty quick. Did you find someone to replace Ivy League Dude?"

I collapsed on the thick mattress and groaned. "Yeah. Ivy League Dude."

"He followed you?"

"Yeah. But he was okay."

She laughed. "Your tone says better than okay. Guess you forgave him, huh?"

"Guess so. Go back to Very Considerate Hot Guy. Mackenzie will never leave you alone if you don't get laid this trip."

There was another deliberate pause and I imagined her glancing at her companion, checking him out. Good for her. Cassie put so much into her studying, she deserved some frolic. "'K. Catch up with you tomorrow."

"Stay safe," I reminded her. Not that Cassie needed reminding, but I still felt like the worried mother hen of the group.

"Always."

I clicked off the phone and stared at the spotless white ceiling. Maybe this trip would end up being a surprise for all of us.

CHAPTER
Seven

Monday
Quinn

"That's your boat?"

My mouth dropped open as I stood on the deck overlooking the huge catamaran with the massive sails tugging in the wind. It looked about forty feet, with gorgeous teak wood and equipment galore. I knew nothing about sailing, rarely venturing into the water except for a quick swim, but I knew this was mega expensive. I had expected a small motorboat we'd tool around in for the day. Should have realized my Ivy Leaguer would impress the hell out of me.

He pushed his sunglasses up on his head and grinned. God, he was gorgeous. The light played on his midnight brown curls and soaked into his tanned skin. Tiny lines crinkled around his full lips as he smiled, and those eyes rivaled any body of water in the world—a searing light blue that lasered right to the soul. He wore white shorts, boating shoes, and a collared blue shirt that stretched over his broad chest and emphasized the powerful muscles of his biceps. Oh my. Thank goodness I had donned the daring red bikini Mackenzie had bought me and I refused previously to wear. Right now, it was hidden discreetly under my black tank top and khaki shorts. With my ponytail and Ked sneakers, I felt about twelve years old next to his masculine yumminess.

"Do you like it?" he asked.

"It's huge." I expected something cozy with just us. Surely this came with a crew.

"I thought bigger was better."

I pursed my lips at his little quip, but couldn't help the laugh that spilled out, and quickly turned into my awful pig snort. I decided to give it back to him a bit. "Big is nice, but you have to know how to use it."

His eyes darkened. "Oh, I know how to use it."

A delicious shiver raced down my spine. I shrugged. "So you say. We'll see."

He laughed and I grinned. I was terrible at flirting, but with James, it felt natural. Like teasing him was part of the fun and the sexual spark. "Brat." He pulled playfully at my ponytail and my scalp tingled. "Got everything you need?"

I showed him my gaily striped beach bag with towel, lotion, bottled water, phone, and a change of clothes. "Where are we going?"

He grabbed the bag and guided me toward the catamaran. "I'll show you some sights first, head down the Gulf. I staked out a pretty place for a swim and a picnic. We'll let the day guide us."

The sheer freedom of those words made me giddy. No plans, no timetable, no responsibilities. How long had it been since I was able to let go? Too long. Emotion choked the back of my throat. "Sounds perfect."

He studied my face, then smiled as if he liked what he saw. "Good. Welcome aboard."

The marina was buzzing with activity and packed with an array of schooners, catamarans, and smaller powerboats. Men yelled back and forth to each other, seagulls screeched in outrage or happiness, and lines formed by booths for private charters and excursions. The sun was blinding and hot, scorching delicate skin and dousing the choppy water with glittering sparkles. James gave me a quick tour, and I was amazed at the amount of space on the boat. A shower, huge cabin, and fully stocked bar was down below. Long teak benches were set up to lay out, and the brilliant white canvas was shocking against the stinging blue of sky.

"Where's the rest of the crew?" I asked.

"Just me. No worries, I've been sailing since I was ten, and I know boats and the water in Key West well. Been coming here a long time. Do you trust me?"

The words meant more than boating, and I knew it. I also knew my answer. "Yes."

His face softened. "Then I won't let you down," he said lightly. "Let me get started and we'll pull out in a few."

I settled down to watch from behind the safety of my sunglasses, sipping from a bottle of water, and admired the ripple of muscles as he moved back and forth and we drifted away from the marina. As the crowds shrank and the noise dimmed, I was taken to another dimension where only nature ruled. I'd only been on a boat once before, a ferry cruise for sightseeing with my dad. The event, as usual, had ended in disaster. I'd begged him to just drink soda, but he snuck to the bar a few times for his beer, got drunk, and fell down the spiral stairs. He only avoided serious injury because he was so inebriated he literally bounced. The humiliation from the public attention was brutal. I'd never gone on another boat since.

But I didn't want to think about the past right now.

I pushed away the memory and concentrated on today.

CHAPTER

James

I wondered what she was thinking about.

Her face darkened, as if a shadow of a bad memory drifted past, and then she seemed to calm again. I wondered about her secrets. She seemed to have everything together, so unlike me, yet something I wanted to probe simmered beneath her surface.

Which was dangerous.

I'd gone to bed last night with a hard dick and had to jerk off twice just to try and get some sleep. One lousy night in her company and she had me whipped. Of course, I knew all the rational explanations. She was different, and once I slept with her, the lure of the chase would settle me. Kind of shitty, but men were pretty much the same. We couldn't really help it—our dicks led our brains and once satisfied, the fog cleared and we were able to think clearly again.

Still, I'd dreamed about her when I finally fell asleep. She was standing by the water, her beautiful dark hair spilling around her shoulders, looking at me with a gentle expression. As if I was important. It was a lake in my dreams—not an ocean—and the sunlight rippled over the water, and I stood before her, wanting to reach out and take her hand, wanting her to belong to me in every way possible, but I froze and didn't know if I could complete the gesture.

Then I woke up.

I concentrated on my tasks, set our course, and began to relax. I'd loved sailing from the first moment I'd set foot on my dad's boat. My parents taught me because it was expected, especially since they took large parties out for charity and business, but the moment I got on the water, I recognized a peace I rarely experienced. Most everything they forced me to do was for them. This was the only time I felt like sailing was just for me. Alone with my thoughts, with strict tasks to achieve direction, it was a melding of creativity and concreteness, a mix of nature and manmade instincts combined to create something close to perfection. Like my art.

I grabbed a bottle of Coke from the cooler and went to Quinn. She propped herself on the edge of the decking, looking out at the horizon, her ponytail swishing back and forth in the breeze. Her breasts were full and high, pushing against the stretchy black tank and begging for my fingers. I remembered how they felt against my chest, perfectly curved with hard nipples, like cherries on a sundae. The shorts barely covered her upper thighs, and my gaze kept sneaking back to the smooth skin and endless length of leg exposed. I imagined them wrapping around my hips and holding me tight. An odd protectiveness mixed with general lust and confused me. Usually things were so clear when I met a girl I intended to sleep with, but Quinn threw me out of whack from the very first meeting.

She looked up and I handed her a bottle of soda. A sweep of red streaked down her arm, and I frowned as I gently touched it. "Where's your sunscreen? You have to be careful; you'll burn easy out here." That milky white skin wasn't made for the Keys, and it was only gonna get sunnier..

Her voice came out husky, like she'd woken up. "In my bag."

The bottle lay on top of her bag, so I scooped it up and squeezed some into my hand. I rubbed the creamy lotion into her shoulders, making sure not to press too hard, and worked the stuff into her skin until the white had disappeared. She held still, not moving, and I took my time enjoying taking care of her, and the silky smoothness under my fingers. "Turn," I said roughly. She blinked and obeyed, and I slowly did her front, over the swell of her breasts, her neck, and knelt down in front of her. She sucked in her breath but didn't move, just waited for me to continue. Never breaking my gaze, I poured more lotion into my palm and lay my hands on her upper thighs where the shorts ended. She began chewing on that lush lower lip I so badly wanted to taste, but I kept moving, working down her sleek thighs, to her knees, calves, and even the top of her feet. With a final squeeze, I rose and stared into her eyes. "I'll reapply when we're ready to swim. Did you bring your suit?"

She nodded. Satisfaction coursed through me. At least she wanted me just as much, evident in her inability to mutter a word and the confused heat in her gorgeous chocolate eyes. I needed to pace myself for the day and not move too fast. I'd be happy to drag her into the cabin right now and keep her naked all day, but I bet that wouldn't go over too well.

At least, not yet.

"Uh-oh. What are you thinking? You look extremely... satisfied."

I grinned. "Really wanna know?"

Her cheeks grew pink. God, she was cute. "Never mind," she muttered. I couldn't help it. I laughed and pulled her into me, holding her tight. She relaxed in my arms like she belonged there and we held each other. When she finally broke away, I caught a worried gleam in her eyes. "How many girls have you taken sailing on break?" I knew she regretted the question by the way she chewed her lip, stuck out her chin, and pretended she didn't care about the answer.

Normally, I would've rolled my eyes and said whatever would make her happy. Women always wanted to know if they were special, or just one in a long line. Usually it was the latter, but the game rules were simple. Never admit it was temporary. Use present tense, make sure they felt safe, and at the end I could honestly say I never promised them a thing. That I never meant to be cruel or take advantage. I had played my part for so many years and been disappointed too many times to change the outcome. Either my friends, a girl, or my parents made me feel like shit, like they needed me to be something else. Smarter, richer, funnier. Better. So, I tried not to get too involved anymore with the outcome, because it always went to shit anyway. *Be cool*, I reminded myself. I had an instinct this woman had the ability to shred my barriers to pieces.

Instead, I did the worst thing possible. I told the truth.

"No one," I said. "I've taken out big groups and my friends. But I've never sailed with just one girl before."

"Why?"

I blinked. Why hadn't I? My boat was a frickin' chick magnet, priming them to drop their panties. "Because I like coming out here alone," I admitted. "It's a place for me to think. Reset. I never thought a woman would fit out here before."

She didn't get mushy or reflect on further feelings. Quinn nodded and sat on the bench, stretching out her long legs and crossing them at the ankles. I reminded myself this was about her seduction, not mine. I settled beside her, lifting her legs and dropping them onto my lap. How the hell did she make Keds sexy? "Have you always lived in Chicago? Is that why you went to that particular university?"

"Yeah, I've lived there my whole life. Never really wanted to move, even though we don't have this." She swept her hand in the air to encompass blue sky and the rush of the water.

"You said you work in rehabilitation or something?"

"I have two jobs. I'm interning in an alcohol abuse program, and I work part time at a senior residence home."

I stared at her. "That's a lot of unglamorous work for someone so young."

She shrugged. "I have issues."

A laugh escaped my lips. She was a pisser. "What type?"

"Obsessive compulsive. Control freak. Classic codependent personality that I had to recover from. You know, some of the classics. What's yours?"

I thought for a minute. "Peter Pan syndrome. Poor little rich boy beliefs. Fear of success. Fear of rejection."

She gave me a thumbs-up sign. "Nice."

I grinned and shook my head. "Why are you a classic codependent?"

That shadow of darkness loomed, but she kept talking. "My dad's an alcoholic. My mom died of cancer when I was really young, and he never recovered. He always had a tendency to drink but kept it in check for my mom."

"How old were you?"

"Eight."

"God, that's young. I'm sorry, Quinn. Sucks the big one."

"Yeah." She seemed deep in thought for a while. I didn't push for more information, but I hoped she'd give me more. Imagining her as a child without a mother and having to take care of her dad was awful. "It started small at first. Beer at night, and I'd find the bottles in the morning. Missing work because he claimed he was sick. Got bad."

I fisted my hands and asked the question I dreaded. "Was he abusive?"

She looked surprised, then laughed. "Oh God, no. Dad was an emotional drunk. Got sloppy, fell down, cried over Mom. Begged my forgiveness. Maybe that's why it seemed even harder. He was always so sorry and swore to never do it again. I just kept believing him, until I stopped questioning his excuses. I kept the secret and helped him function. Classic codependence."

"What happened when you got older?"

She remained still, as if images played on a screen before her. "Things got worse. We had little money since he couldn't keep a job. Unemployment ran out. I worked on the side, but with school I was limited. Then he started having me apply for credit cards. We'd get these preapproved offers in the mail in my name, and I filled out every one. Do you know at eighteen years old I had almost fifteen thousand dollars in credit? And I was wiped out at nineteen because he'd used up everything but begged for more."

I reached out and snagged her hand. Squeezed. She seemed startled out of her reflections, and my heart split at the sight of her face. She was beyond beautiful. She was strong and brave. "You had nobody to help you?" I asked.

"No. But I reached rock bottom along with him. Broke and dead tired. Trying to keep everything together was killing me. I reached out to Al-Anon and for me, everything changed. I realized I couldn't protect him from himself, that I was actually helping him drink. I met people involved in the program—people like me, and I confronted him. Had an intervention and moved out."

"What happened?"

"He fell apart. Begged me to help. I refused. That was the hardest part, realizing he had to do it himself. Had to want to stop the cycle. Eventually, he went to rehab, and he's been sober now for almost a year."

"And you? How are you?"

A ghost of a smile touched her lips. "Better. Paying off my debt. I love my jobs because my work helps people, and it makes sense. I take it day by day a lot, just like my dad. He's making amends and seems happy. That's all I ever wanted. For us to be okay and happy."

Isn't that what I searched for day-to-day, too? To be at peace with my emotions that always seemed to torment, reminding me I was nothing in a world of everything? The pain clawed for daylight, but I struck it back down and locked it up. Quinn was beyond me. She owned character and had no one helping her. I had a pot full of money, opportunities everywhere, and I still failed.

The shame was bitter and almost choked me. I raised her palm to my lips and kissed her fingers. "You amaze me. The people at those centers are lucky to have you." I kept my gaze firmly averted so she couldn't find out the truth too soon, and lifted her legs to slide out. "I better check the route. Be right back."

I hid behind the sails, confirmed our direction, and wondered if I'd ever be worthy of someone like her—or anyone, for that matter.

CHAPTER

Quinn

He moved like a dancer around the boat, his hands deft and capable on the riggings and manipulating the pathway so it seemed he was in control of the actual wind. Odd, I shared more with him than I ever had with another guy. It just seemed right, as if secrets on the water would drift away until I felt clean. But there was something in his eyes that made me feel he hid something. Like it was okay for me to share, but not him.

I sighed and took a sip of Coke. I could've killed myself for asking about other women. I mean, how lame was that? Like he was going to say, "No, there was no one else before you." I wanted to take it back so bad, but when he told me he hadn't taken out another woman, I actually believed him. I don't know why it was important, but it was. It should be about sex and nothing else, but my damn emotions always got a bit involved, and I needed to feel safe.

No wonder Mackenzie always yelled at me.

The catamaran slid into shore and James docked the boat in a tiny space that seemed to be created just for us. I looked around, but there was no one else on the mini island retreat. He took a while to get set up, and then he faced me with a big smile on his face. "Welcome to my own private island."

Huh? My mouth fell open. "You're kidding me."

"Yes." He tugged my ponytail again and laughed. "Sorry, I couldn't help it. Let's just say not many people come out here, and I grease a few palms of the main sightseeing crews to keep it that way. It's safe to do some swimming, and I brought a picnic. It's just us."

Excitement shimmered and danced on my nerve endings. He loomed over me, tall and gorgeous, those curls blowing in the wind, smelling of sea, and salt, and man. "Sounds good."

"Let's get set up." He grabbed my bag, a basket, some towels, and a bottle of champagne. We stepped out onto the tiny ridge and made our way to the main piece of the island. It was mostly rock, with a large strip of sand, so we settled ourselves right in the center. As he unpacked, I investigated the space. Surrounded by jagged rocks, the water rushed on the surf and left behind an array of broken shells. I walked around the edges, tracing the lines, and stared out at the vast expanse of water and sky before me.

"We're inside the barrier reef," he said from behind me. "Completely safe. Good for snorkeling too, if you're interested. I brought the equipment."

I adjusted my sunglasses to avoid the glare and looked up. "I'm not huge into water sports, but I may give it a try. This is beautiful. I feel like we're alone in the world."

"Yeah, problems get more manageable when you're around nature. It's a reminder there's something bigger than you, and somehow, everything works out."

His words startled me. He liked to play at being the drop out-spoiled-rich kid, but his words haunted me like poetry.

Way more sophisticated than the usual twenty-something guy. There was a lot more underneath the surface I was dying to unearth. "I'm starving," I moaned.

"Good. 'Cause you'll need your energy."

The sexual spark zinged between us and stole my breath. His blue eyes darkened as if he knew exactly what I was feeling, but he only led me back to the blanket that was spread out. The food was simple, just like I enjoyed. Roast beef sandwiches, salad, strawberries, and champagne. He uncorked the bottle and the pleasant pop made me laugh, especially when the liquid bubbled and spilled on top of him. He filled up two plastic flutes and tapped his glass to mine.

"To the day."

I smiled. "To the day." I sipped and purred with enjoyment. I loved champagne, but only drank it on New Year's Eve. Always seemed too decadent. I slipped off my Keds and dug my toes in the sand.

"Were your friends okay with you coming to meet me today?" he asked, biting into his sandwich.

"Yeah, I spoke with them this morning. Mackenzie won't let us hang out together. Says we'll never meet anybody new. She's trying to get Cassie and me out of our comfort zones."

He frowned. "She looked so familiar. The one with the hat, right?"

I hesitated, but I was already too far gone and trusted him enough to keep our secret. "Yeah. Country music star."

He snapped his fingers. "That's it! Been driving me crazy. Damn, how'd you get to be friends with Mackenzie Forbes? She's been in the public eye since she was young."

"She goes to Chicago State. Cassie and I met her in English 101. I don't know, we just clicked. I'd trust her with my life, and she's looking for some normalcy away from the country circuit." I stared at him. "You won't tell anyone, right?"

James shook his head. "No, I promise to keep it quiet."

"Thanks. She doesn't need the paparazzi ruining her vacation. How about your friends? Have you known those guys long?"

"I'm probably the closest to Rich and Adam. We travel in the same circles. Our parents know each other; we went to the fancy schools and country clubs and tennis lessons together. Weird, you think the world is big, but when you're growing up, it's pretty damn small. I only met kids my parents approved of. I didn't know most of the other people. They're all casual acquaintances who like my money and stuff."

He stated the words like it was no big deal, but I knew it was. How must it feel to have everything given to you and still not be happy? Because that's how he struck me, as if he had to apologize for his lifestyle all the time. It was a different way to look at it. I'd longed for money many times, but never thought of the way it could take away your freedom. I always believed it gave more options and choices. Evidently, not for James. At least, not in the past.

"What about now? You're over twenty-one. You can make your own way now, right?"

"Sure. I do what I want, when I want. I have the perfect life."

Lie. He refused to look at me. My stomach clenched with the need to make him face me, but he definitely didn't want to have a heart-to-heart. Whatever. This was about sex, not confessions. In a few days, I'd be back on a plane to Chicago and he'd be only a memory. I needed to make sure it was a good one.

"Sorry," I muttered. "See? I get pushy. Issues."

His face softened and a smile tugged at his lips. God, when he smiled my insides melted like goo and an ache twitched between my thighs. "I like that about you. You look cool and collected on the surface, but there's this fire when you look deeper."

"So you're saying I'm hot?"

He laughed and so did I. "Hell, yeah," he said softly. "Hotter than Hades, baby."

I refused to blush and concentrated on cleaning up the

remains of our lunch. We repacked the basket, and left out the champagne. "What's next?" I blurted out.

A wolfish grin transformed his mouth. Fascinated, I watched as he grabbed the neckline of my tank and tugged me toward him. His gaze focused on my mouth, and I had the urge to bite my lip, which was so fucking cliché I hated it, but it was a childhood habit I'd never gotten over.

"The only thing left to do," he drawled. "Strip."

CHAPTER

James

The laughter died in my throat. Her eyes widened and a shocked gasp dropped from her lips, but the sudden image of Quinn naked in front of me wiped out the joke. My voice felt rusty. "We're gonna swim, right?"

Recognition hit. She scrunched up her nose and gave me a halfhearted punch on my arm. "Very funny."

"Mind in the gutter much?" She blushed and I pressed a hard kiss against her soft lips. "Sorry, I couldn't help it. I like when you get embarrassed."

"I'm not! I don't!"

"'K." I ran a finger down her heated cheek, and she jerked her head with a muttered curse. She tipped the last drops of her champagne, set it aside, and began wiggling out of her tank top.

And that's when I realized the joke was on me.

Fuck. The black cotton tank eased over her head and got dropped to the sand. With a wicked glance from under her lashes, she flicked open the button on her khaki shorts, dragged down the zipper, and slid the material down her legs.

My dick wept for mercy. Every muscle tightened as I fought for control. The red bikini should have been illegal. The top was just two tiny squares covering her breasts, and the bottom had a sexy string on each hip that made me fantasize about slowly unlooping it to see what was hidden beneath. Her skin was pale and flawless, stretched like a gift across toned muscle and endless legs. The swing of her ponytail was pure sass as she grinned at me. "This good?"

"Witch," I muttered. "How am I supposed to concentrate?" I looked down at my demanding erection. "Thank God there's no audience. You officially got me back."

She stuck out her tongue and bounded toward the water.

Her full ass was barely covered as she dove in and surfaced, shaking off the water and gasping for breath. "It's so warm. Come on in."

My hands paused on my belt buckle. Shit. I had planned to change on the boat but got distracted. I longed to just get naked and skinny-dip, but I didn't want to shock her. I pulled out my bathing suit from beneath the towel and held it up. "I still have to change. Turn around."

Her delighted laugh echoed in the water. She swam closer. "Hmm, this is an interesting dilemma. Be good and give you privacy? Or be bad and get a preview?"

Her sense of humor challenged me. Who would've thought she was so snarky and fun? I decided to play a game of chicken. "You want a preview, huh? Well, hold on, baby girl. Here you go."

I pulled off my T-shirt and tossed it away. Her gaze roved over my naked chest and turned me on even more. I couldn't wait until her hands were all over me. I dropped my hands back to my belt, loosened the leather, and pulled the metal lever open. Grasped the zipper. And waited.

"I'm not wearing underwear."

She squealed and whipped around fast, presenting me with her lovely back. I laughed and dropped my shorts, taking my time to change into my bathing suit in order to torture her a bit. When I managed to squeeze myself into the suit with an uncomfortable erection, I hit the water with a splash and swam toward her.

She laughed and tried to kick me away, but I was a strong swimmer and always believed I was part fish. I dove under, grabbed her legs, and yanked her up so she was firmly secured in my arms. Her wet skin slid over mine, and her nipples poked against the thin red material from the water. And hopefully something else.

"Round one to me," I said.

"Were you teasing?" she asked suspiciously.

"You'll never know. Next time you'll have to take the risk."

She wrinkled her nose in annoyance, but allowed me to hold her. All my circuits were firing nonstop, my body attuned to each curve pressed against mine. Suddenly, she wrapped her arms around my shoulders and clung tight. I fought a groan, wondering if I'd drown in her sweetness. "James?"

"Yeah?"

"I know another game we can play."

My heart slammed against my chest and I tightened my hold. *Oh yeah.* "Sounds intriguing. What's the game?"

Her legs brushed against my thighs and her breath rushed over my lips. "It's called Catch Me if You Can."

I came way too close to untying that cute bow from her hip, hooking my finger under the bottoms, and diving deep. "Rules?"

Her voice was hot and dripped over me like an ice cream cone on a summer day. "There's only one. You have to count to one hundred before you chase me."

I almost passed out but managed to rally. "Done. What do I get when I find you?"

Her lips touched mine in a whisper soft kiss. "Anything

you want."

Oh, she was killing me. "How do we start?"

"Close your eyes. Count to one hundred. Then try to catch me."

My eyes drifted close with the promise of pleasure ahead. She broke the embrace, and I heard her dive under the water.

That's when she yanked down my bathing suit.

It happened so fast, I couldn't get my bearings. In a flash, she was swimming away, and I fought the natural urge to go after her, but I remembered the rules of the game and kept my eyes shut, continuing to count. Her musical laughter drifted to my ears, and I realized I hadn't had so much fun with a woman in a long, long time. Who would've thought such mischief lurked beneath her serious facade?

I played fair and got to one hundred. When I opened my eyes a surge of adrenalin and lust mingled and exploded. I sank back into primitive time, knowing once I hunted her she'd be mine, on my terms.

She'd definitely left the water, there weren't even bubbles around, and I was stuck naked. Thoughts of sweet revenge kept me focused as I trudged out of the water and began exploring the small island for clues. I grabbed a towel and wrapped it around my waist, peeking behind rocks and looking for a path to follow.

The water droplets pooled together in a large wet patch led me back to the boat.

Sneaky girl. I made sure to remain silent as I reboarded and made my way in an organized search. My wet bathing suit had been dropped onto the bench. I checked the cabin and bathroom, opened doors, and finally heard a squeak.

I caught a flash of red and I dove for her. She tried to rush past me to get back off the boat and run to the island, but I leapt at the last moment and tackled her around the waist. She let out a terrified yelp and tried to fight me, but I kept my balance and tossed her over my shoulder in one smooth motion. My hand caught her flailing legs and kept her still.

"Let me go!" she yelled, squirming in a way that set me off.

"Not a chance. I caught you fair and square. It's payback time. Head down, sweetheart." I climbed down the stairs to the main cabin, making sure I ducked so she didn't hit herself on the ceiling ledge, and headed toward the bedroom.

The mattress was large and comfortable, even though the room was a bit on the small side. I lowered her down flat on her back, climbed on top of her, and straddled her. My towel fell off. I kept my hands off her so if she panicked, I could roll right off, but she responded immediately to my show of domination and stopped struggling. My gaze locked on hers.

Pupils were dilated. Her pulse pounded, evident at the base of her neck. She panted for breath, and her nipples were hard points beneath her bikini top, begging for me to pull down the fabric and take them in my mouth. Yeah, she was definitely into this. I just needed to be careful she didn't get spooked, and make sure she was ready for me.

"I caught you."

"I guess." She stared right back, unblinking. "What are you going to do with me?"

I grinned. Her body spread before me like a feast I was about to devour, but I needed to go slow, or it would be over way too soon. She deserved an orgasm she'd never forget. I craved to wipe out every guy she had before me and replace them with my face.

Slowly, I lowered myself, giving her the opportunity to wrench free or tell me to stop. She didn't. Her eyes darkened to an inky black. My hands slid up her naked belly and cupped her breasts. Quinn gave a low moan and arched her back. I tweaked the hard tips with my thumbs, enjoying her open response, and shifted my weight so I knelt over her, my mouth close to hers.

"Everything, Quinn. I'm going to do...everything."

I took her mouth in a fierce kiss, finally letting myself go and refusing to hold back. She was right there with me, opening her lips to my tongue as I drank her in and conquered the wet silk of her mouth. I kept up the tweaks to her nipples, refusing to go underneath her top, even though her body begged for more. My erection throbbed for relief, but I was afraid too much pressure against my dick would get me off. Shit, I felt like a teen with my first woman, so I locked my brain down with my control and swore to give her the most pleasure I could.

I sucked on her lips and nibbled on the bottom, giving her a sharp bite. She bucked underneath me. "Oh yeah, you like that," I murmured, pulling at her nipples and twisting a bit. "What else do you like, baby? I want to find all of it, every secret your body tries to hide."

Her lips were slick and swollen, like a bee sting. I worked my way down her neck, nibbling and licking, until I finally reached her covered breasts. One quick tug and the top fell down, exposing her fully. Crap, she was amazing. Small, perfectly formed, with tight red nipples I wanted to suck for hours. She reached up and hung on to my hair, tugging slightly, as I lashed at her nipples with my tongue.

"James! Oh God, that feels so good!"

"You taste so sweet," I groaned. I massaged her hips and belly as I worked her breasts until she writhed back and forth in a frenzy. "Are you wet for me?"

She shuddered and I decided to find out for myself. My fingers closed around the cute little bows and I pulled one of the strings until one side loosened. Drawing small circles around her hipbone, I teased her, loving the way she whimpered and tried to get closer. She smelled like coconut lotion and musky arousal, my favorite combination. I moved to the other side and tugged.

Then removed her bottoms.

I sucked in my breath. Holy shit, I wasn't gonna last much longer. Her pussy gleamed with wetness, and she'd waxed for the beach so only a fine strip of dark hair was left. The perfect landing strip for my mouth and fingers. She flushed and tried to get up, probably caught between arousal and embarrassment.

"You're so fucking beautiful, Quinn. Do you know that? Do know how bad I want you?" I grabbed her hand and pressed her fingers over my dick. Already, the tip was leaking with my arousal. "You make me crazy. I want to make you feel good, make you come so hard against me, make you scream. Let me, baby. Let me in. Part your legs."

She hissed out a breath, but she was too far gone, so she obeyed. Her lips were plump and moist, and I ran a finger around her labia, watching her clench and lift her hips for more. I leaned over and blew my breath over the tight, damp curls, spread my palms flat against her inner thighs, and dove into heaven.

She cried out as I kissed her, licked her clit around and around, harnessing all her sexual arousal until she was completely under my control and begging me. My name echoed in the air, the sweetest fucking sound I ever heard, and I closed my lips around her clit and sucked hard.

She came in my mouth, bucking like crazy, and I helped her ride it out. Fierce satisfaction coursed through me, but I couldn't wait any longer. I fumbled madly for the drawer beside the bed, and managed to grab a condom with my shaking fingers. Her scent dripped over me like nectar, and she was still shuddering with tiny convulsions. I ripped open the wrapper, rolled on the condom, and poised by her entrance.

Her gorgeous dark eyes were blurry from her climax. Her lids drifted half closed. "Look at me, Quinn," I demanded. I wanted to see every part of her, and she obeyed, gasping as I pushed a few inches into her clingy heat. "Mine." Possession beat through me in waves. Rational thought had long fled, and I was down to a primitive state, where I needed to claim her and have her belong only to me. Her gaze locked on mine.

I surged forward.

Hot and wet, her pussy clenched around me and sucked me deep. I fought for control as I pushed all the way, holding her legs wide open, and my body shook with tremors of pleasure. She moaned and grabbed at my shoulders, the sting of her nails biting deep into my skin and urging me on. My hips pulled back and I slid out of her completely, then thrust in hard. Harder.

She threw back her head and screamed as I pounded into her body over and over, brutal and raw, needing to mark her as mine, mine, mine. I felt her milk my dick as she came again, and I let myself go with a long yell, spilling my seed into the condom and bucking my hips, drawing out as much of the pleasure as I could. She whimpered, shaking in my embrace, and I slumped over her, panting for breath, my skin damp with sweat, my cock still inside her.

I had no idea how long we stayed like that. I finally realized I might be crushing her, so I rolled to the side and she dropped her head onto my chest. If someone forced me to stand up, my legs would never hold. Every muscle in my body was loose and used. Fuck. I'd never experienced such a powerful orgasm in my life.

I was in deep shit. This woman was addicting.

"*That* was intense," Quinn finally said.

I laughed and cuddled her tight. "Baby, you blew my mind. Forget the rest of the week. I'm keeping you right here."

She smiled and looked up. "Sounds like a plan." My heart melted at the sight of her face. Such a mix of seriousness and play; intellect and character. She was amazing, and she was mine for the next few days. I couldn't think of anything past the moment. Didn't want to.

"James?"

"Yeah, baby?"

"That was the best game ever."

I grinned.

CHAPTER
Eleven

Quinn

I laid in the bed naked, sheets twisted half around my legs. James pinned me to the mattress with one heavy thigh slung over my hips, dozing after our last bout of amazing, mind-numbing, pleasure-ridden sex.

My lips turned in a dazed smile and the mantra sang over and over in my head.

I had an orgasm. I had an orgasm. Quinn Harmon had an orgasm. Yay, yay, yay.

No wonder everyone was obsessed! Sex without orgasms was okay. The cuddling was the best part. But *with* an orgasm? The whole encounter rocked. My body was sluggish and melty, like gooey caramel oozing all over the place. There was only one downside: They were kind of like potato chips. Now that I had one—oh, actually three—I wanted more. I'd never go back to sex without orgasms. Which meant James may have ruined me for life. In a good way.

The other weird thing was my usual shyness completely dissipated. Maybe it was the way he looked at me. As if he found me gorgeous and refused to let me hide. I wasn't a huge fan of my small breasts and boyish-type figure, but he made me feel like a goddess. I would've never been bold enough to play a little hide-and-go sex game before. Maybe this whole spring break thing allowed me to leave my regular self behind and be someone I always wanted to be. Someone more like Mackenzie—bold and sexy and able to go after what she wanted.

"What are you thinking about?"

His growly voice drifted to my ears and my body gave an involuntary shudder. Oh yeah, he had me whipped good. I was like a trained puppy now, ready to do anything to get my next orgasm. He'd created a monster. His hands reached out and stroked my naked hip, tracing my pubic bone, and finally resting warm on my stomach.

"Sex. With you," I admitted.

"My favorite subject." His hand trailed lower, pointing toward the magic spot, but he stilled his motions. I tried not to wriggle. "I refuse to become the ultimate cliché and ask how it was for you." His fingers played me like a musical instrument, gliding over my skin in teasing strokes but never dipping low enough. "I'd rather watch your reaction to know I'm pleasing you."

I blushed. Guess some of my natural reserve couldn't be banished. His gaze stripped me bare, probed me deep, and left me nowhere to hide. I grew wet and my nipples pebbled for his attention. It was like I wasn't in control of my own body anymore—it all belonged to him. And it's exactly the way I liked it.

"Look at you," he whispered. "All pink and wet. I'd be happy to keep you stripped and tied to my bed for the rest of the week." He propped himself up on his side and caressed my breast, rubbing his thumb over my tight nipple over and over again, making it swell and push out for more. He was so dirty and sexy and raw. He rolled over and began to lick me all over, wet swipes of his tongue mingling with tiny nibbles that made me squirm. "Now part your legs for me, Quinn. No, open your eyes."

My lids flew open at his command. Somehow, if I was able to hide from my own response, it would've been safer, but he didn't let me. He wanted it all, and I ached to give it to him. I spread my thighs wide, helpless and ready to beg for what I wanted, no longer caring who I was before I met him. "So pretty," he murmured. He swiped a finger down my slit and I sucked in my breath. His blue eyes darkened to navy, sucking me as deep as my pussy pulled in his finger, begging for more. "I'm going to make you come again. Don't close your eyes. This is all for me, Quinn, do you hear me?"

"Yes," I moaned. "Please."

He dipped a finger in, stretched me, then added another. His thumb brushed my clit with light teasing touches that never gave me the pressure I needed. I arched up for more, but he was in complete control, watching my naked body and my face with raw satisfaction. His fingers curled and he pumped in and out with slow strokes. The pleasure built and swam in waves around me, and then—

"Oh God!" He hit a spot that shimmered raw streams of bliss through my body. I panted hard, wanting more, wanting less, wanting...

"That's the spot. Give me more, baby. Show me how good this feels."

He began a rhythmic thrust back and forth in that magic place, and my muscles tightened with anticipation, building higher and higher until I felt as I would scream or shatter. I flailed my head back and forth on the pillow and closed my eyes to fight off the pressure.

"Open your eyes. Don't hide from me."

I moaned as I obeyed, and his fingers moved faster, his thumb rubbing, and then the orgasm hit me, shimmering from the tight coil in my belly and flooding every pore with a light and energy that made me scream at the top of my lungs. I heard him cursing in the background, fumbling with a drawer, but my senses were swamped with too much stimuli, and then I felt his sheathed hard length slide into me.

"So good," I cried brokenly. "So good."

"You were made for me. Jesus, your body is so tight and hot. I can't get enough of you." He worked his hips and drove me right back up, his fingers clenching my ass and holding me still for every stroke, and I gave myself up to him, letting him do what he wanted and take me anywhere. The pressure rebuilt and I shattered into a second orgasm—my ass bruised, my thighs shaking, and throat raw from my screams. He came hard and threw his head back, shouting my name and collapsed on top of my body.

I had no idea how much time passed before I was able to move. Like coming out of a Rip Van Winkle sleep, the room seemed foggy and my body was limp from use. The scent of sex and a delicious musky cologne filled the air. I wondered if I'd ever walk properly again, or if I was permanently bow-legged.

"Wanna take a shower?" he asked, stroking back my tangled hair. My ponytail had come free at some point.

"Yes, please." I wrinkled my nose. "I'm a mess."

"You're a gorgeous mess," he corrected, dropping a kiss on my nose. "I have robes in the closet. Get comfortable and meet me on the deck. I'm gonna clean up a bit and get ready to sail back."

"What time is it?"

He grinned. "Almost sunset."

I gasped. "We spent the whole day in bed?" I'd heard of couples doing that before but always figured it was an exaggeration. After all, how many hours can you actually have sex? Now I knew.

"Yep. I'll take you on a sunset sail. We have some leftover sandwiches and champagne. Meet me upstairs when you're ready."

I watched him climb out of bed. HIs body was a work of supple, defined muscles, a tight ass, and meaty biceps. Dusky tanned skin covered with dark hair. Even his feet seemed strong and sensual. He donned a T-shirt, pair of shorts, and with a wink, climbed the stairs. I slumped back onto the pillows.

Best. Spring. Break. Ever.

I took my time getting cleaned up and back in my suit. The terry cloth robe felt snug and comfy. I made my way to the upper deck, and found a small table set up with the remains of our lunch and more champagne. The sails whipped in the wind, and the landscape seemed distant and far, far away. The sun was a giant ball of fire, suspended halfway in the sky, and I gasped at the outrageous beauty. The moment was idyllic, almost from a dream. James seemed to experience similar emotions, because he moved over and wrapped me in his arms. Nothing mattered anymore. It was just us—free and alone on the water, and our boat chasing the sun.

"Is it always like this?" I murmured against his chest. My cheek rubbed against soft worn cotton, and I leaned into his strength.

He paused. I waited for him to ask what my question meant. I wasn't sure myself. But his voice whispered on the wind and drifted to my ears. "No. It's usually never like this."

We didn't speak for a while. I realized something strong surged between us, beyond the sex, but it was too massive and complicated to analyze now. I worried about so much in my life, I didn't want to turn my perfect encounter with James into something to pick apart and rationalize.

We broke apart and sat down. I was starving, and ripped into the rest of the roast beef and salad without taking a breath. He laughed at me and refilled my champagne glass. "How long do you usually stay in Key West?" I asked curiously.

He shrugged. "Usually after break is over, I move on. Sometimes I stay a week or two longer, depending on my plans."

I hated the doubts that suddenly sprang to mind. He probably seduced a girl each year, kept her for the week, then moved on. And wasn't my goal the same thing? So stupid. I had gotten attached after one lousy day in his bed. I'd make a terrible casual lover. I stiffened my resolve to make sure I didn't make it more than it was, or pressure him in any way. Even after his words that this seemed to mean a bit more than an easy roll in the hay. "Sounds perfect," I said lightly, finishing up my food.

"It is sometimes," he said. He watched me from across the table with a brooding gaze. "But sometimes it's just…empty."

My gaze cut to his. Heat blazed and blistered. It didn't matter that we'd been at each other all day. My body flamed back to life, hungry for more. He muttered a curse but kept still in his seat. "Empty how?" I questioned.

He stiffened. Anger seemed to beat from his figure, confusing me. "I do what I want, when I want. I make my own schedule, travel anywhere in the world, and have enough money and security not to worry. But there's no one on the other end. If I dropped off the face of the earth, no one would give a shit."

I sucked in my breath. The sudden vulnerability in his features fisted my heart and squeezed. How could that be possible? James Hunt had everything. Didn't he? "Your parents? Friends? Siblings, cousins?"

His profile remained carved in stone. "I'm an only child. I was pretty much raised by my housekeeper, private tutors, and learned everything needed to be the perfect society boy. It wasn't until later that I began to question my role."

"What role?"

"I was a prop. My parents only wanted one child so they could raise it to be what they needed. They'd sweep in to parade me in front of their friends, or at a party, or to show off. Most of the time they barely spoke with me, unless it was with demands on who I could see, how I should behave, all that crap." His voice became distant and cold. "When I figured out fucking up would at least bring their wrath, that was good enough for me. At least I got some reaction at first. Dad focused on getting me some reputable career or drafting me into the banking empire, but he doesn't get it. I'd die. I tried talking to him about it, but he didn't give a shit. Neither did Mom. So they gave up on me, released my trust fund money, and threatened to disown me if I humiliated them."

"I'm sure they didn't mean it. Parents threaten things all the time."

Shadows flickered over his face. "No. They meant it. They check up on me, of course. Skype, text, an occasional call. But not to really talk or find out what I'm up to. They want to be sure I haven't done anything to wreck the family name. My last visit was a clusterfuck. I got an hour at breakfast, and they both cited shit excuses to avoid me the rest of the weekend. I have no other family—they were both only children—and my friends? As I told you, they like what I can give them but if I had no money, they wouldn't stick."

"Maybe you never give them a chance?" I suggested gently. "I'm sure they'd care about you whether or not you had buckets of money."

He laughed, but it was bitter and without humor. "You still don't get it, do you, Quinn? I'm a complete mirage. Underneath, there's nothing there. I go from one event to another, one place to the next. My friends just happen to be the ones I take with me for the ride, and when I drop them off, they happily leave. I'm a fucking ghost. Maybe it's good. No one gets hurt. No complications. Easy in, easy out."

"Why are you telling me this?" My voice trembled. There was something greater growing between us; a seed that sprouted and would soon become Jack's beanstalk with just a bit of care and tenderness. But how could such a connection happen in a day? Was that even possible? Or was I living in my own mirage, with no responsibilities and reality to intrude in perfection?

His eyes blazed. "So you know. You need to know who I

am, what type of person you're with. I'm not like you. I never will be like you. Do you understand?"

My hand shook around the glass. "You don't know anything about me," I whispered. "Don't try to tell me what I can and can't handle."

He rose from the chair and clenched his fists. I swallowed as a rush of sexual energy punched the air. "You take care of people. Forgive them. You're strong and real, and I don't want you to forget it. But at the end of this week, you're gonna get on that plane and walk away. Without me."

My cheeks flamed. How dare he? "Don't flatter yourself," I said coldly. "I'm not a naive little virgin who's going to beg to stay with you. I have a life back in Chicago, and just because we have great sex doesn't mean I'll drop everything to be your groupie. You're a conceited asshole if you think it does."

He shut his eyes tight and seemed to struggle with something deeper. I waited, ready to walk away, ready to fight. His low voice stole my breath and my need to retreat. "That warning isn't for you, little girl." His eyes flew open and blazed hot and fierce. "It's for me."

Raw sexual energy swarmed between us. I knew he was admitting something he didn't want to, and had no idea how to process. He was messing with my head, big time, and I was getting sick of it. "What the hell does that mean anyway?" I hissed.

Emotion tightened my throat at the look of his face. Pain. Frustration.

Vulnerability.

"Damn you," he whispered. "Why'd you have to come here and fuck everything up?"

"Fuck you." I spun on my heel with the intention of getting the hell away from him, but his fingers grasped my arm and yanked me back. He lifted me up. His gaze raked over my face, studying me so intently I felt stripped and naked.

"Don't you get it?" His voice shook. "You're too good for me, Quinn. Soon you're going to see it and leave. And I'll be the one left behind."

Shock held me immobile, but he didn't wait for me to process. He slammed his mouth over mine in a fierce kiss. His grip gentled and he hoisted me up. I groaned and opened my mouth to his thrusting tongue, wrapping my legs tight around his hips as he ripped off my robe. I speared my fingers into his hair and pulled hard, and with a rough curse, he walked me a few steps until my back slammed against the wall. Our mouths drank hungrily from each other, biting, sucking, like two animals crazed to mate, and he must've grabbed a condom from his pocket, because I was suddenly sinking on top of him and he filled me completely.

"Ahhh!" A cry ripped from my mouth. His cock was huge and thick, piercing right through my body and filling it up, until there was no space or thought or safe place from him. He held my hips and roughly guided me up and down, my head scraping the wall, my teeth biting deep into my lower lip and drawing blood. The sensations cut and wracked through my body like knives shredding flesh, and the pleasure became so fierce it was almost pain. My pussy clenched tight, and then I was coming, coming so hard and fast I thought I'd die with the agony of such release, and he was shouting my name and coming with me.

He didn't let go, holding me tight, kissing me gently and caressing my cheeks, telling me I was beautiful and magnificent and that I was everything.

And I knew something had changed. A portal had opened within my soul, and it was all for him, for as long as he wanted me. And I knew I was stupid for thinking we could work out, but I didn't care, so I held him tight and let him care for me, and pretended this was forever.

CHAPTER

Tuesday
Quinn

C made my way into the dining room, trying hard to walk
normally, even though my muscles ached. Of course, this
workout was tons better than any treadmill, and I couldn't wait
to do it again. James had dropped me off at the hotel late last
night, and we made plans to sightsee today.

I scanned the crowd for my tribe and spotted them in
the back booth. Mac's sunhat took up half the table with the
elaborate brim, so I slid next to Cassie. Hmm, she looked tired,
her gray eyes a bit too serious this morning, and not sporting
the afterglow of someone who'd had great sex. Mac looked
like her usual vivacious self. Maybe she scored with her hottie
tattoo guy.

I wondered if my crew would notice I finally had an
orgasm. I felt different. Did I look different? Oh God, I was

so lame.

"You sure about that?" Mac asked.

I picked up the conversation and the menu. "Sure about what?"

"Cassie's fallen in love," Mac announced.

"Oh. Good for her." Did I want an omelets or pancakes?

"No, not good! He has another girlfriend."

"Bastard." I turned to Cassie. "What are you doing messing around with a guy who belongs to someone else?"

"I'm not messing around with him! I can't even get him to kiss me, let alone do anything more." Oh. Well, I couldn't get mad at her for that. "So, not a problem then." Yep, definitely carbs this morning. I deserved them.

Mackenzie gave a long, dramatic sigh. "Problem. This was supposed to be a relaxing vacation. Nobody was supposed to fall in love."

"I'm not in love!" Cassie hissed.

"I don't think you can decide that kind of thing ahead of time," I pointed out. "Especially not for someone else." After all, I didn't know what was going on with James, but I'd never experienced such a strong connection before. I was done judging other people. "I think I'll have pancakes. With blueberries."

"Do they have cheese grits here?" Mackenzie grabbed for the menu. "How about biscuits and gravy? And sweet tea?"

Grits. Yuck.

"This is the South. I wouldn't be surprised," Cassie said. "Just as long as there's orange juice, I'll be happy."

"It's Florida," I said. "There'll be orange juice." I leaned back and got the rest of the dirty lowdown on Cassie and the guy she was attracted to but had a girlfriend. Damn, I wanted her to be able to enjoy herself and let go a little. We were alike, and found it harder to party and leave behind our worries. I urged her to find another guy to take his place, but she didn't seem too thrilled with the promise. Maybe James had someone I could introduce her to. Nah, I didn't care for his friends and wouldn't trust them with Cassie. Especially since she seemed extra paranoid about going around with strangers, citing date rape and all sorts of scary things. I had to remind them all again of their pinky promises to watch our drinks carefully. When I was finally satisfied, I settled into blueberry-and-carb bliss.

Hot tattoo guy was named Austin, and worked as a bartender at Captain Crow's. Mac seemed pretty into him, but when I waited for the big reveal, she only said he'd let it slip that he knew who she was.

"Your turn, Quinn," Mac demanded, shoveling grits into her mouth. For someone so damn skinny, she had a crazy appetite. "What happened with Ivy League Dude? Cassie said he followed you out of the bar and you gave him another chance."

I wondered how much to spill. Who would've thought serious, shy little old me would be getting some before everyone else? I chewed frantically at my lip and tried to decide. Of course, I kept nothing from my best friends, so I found the words tumbling out of my mouth before I could snap them back.

"We went sailing yesterday. I had an orgasm."

Mac spit out her grits and choked. Cassie's eyes widened with admiration. I blushed.

"Woot! That's my girl!" She high-fived me in the booth and glowed with satisfaction. "Was it amazing?"

"Yeah," I sighed. "It was. Now I know what the fuss is all about."

Mac pointed her fork across the table. "Remember, no love shit. Just sex."

Cassie groaned. "What a nightmare. I'm not in love!"

I shot her a sympathetic look. When Mac got on a tear, it was all over. "Sorry, Cass. Of course, the sex is off the charts, but he's completely opposite of anyone I imagined myself with. He flunked out of a bunch of Ivy League schools, has a ton of money, and spends his time throwing parties and travelling the world."

Guilt nipped at my nerves. All of it was true, but I wasn't telling my friends the real stuff. Like how he held me tight, and stroked my hair, and whispered how beautiful I was. How he opened up and admitted there was something between us. How he showed his hurt and loneliness from not having parents or family who gave a crap. I opened my mouth to defend him, but Mac was already talking.

"Who cares? We're here a week, as long as the sex is good and you like him, that's all you need. Anything else is a major complication, and you have enough of those at home, Quinn."

"Yeah. I guess." She was right. I needed to enjoy every moment but try to keep my heart locked up. Falling for James would be a mistake that would get me nowhere but a lot of pain. I spent the rest of the time chatting with Mac. I couldn't help the worry that cut through me. If anyone realized she was America's country sweetheart, we'd be outed and stuck with public scrutiny. Exactly what we all didn't need. Cassie looked even more freaked out than me.

"That's not good, Mac. What if he tells someone, or sells the story of you two?"

Mac shook my head. "He won't."

My brow furrowed. Mac had great instincts, so if she trusted him, I probably would. "You're sure?" I asked.

Mac shrugged. "If he was going to sell me out, don't you think the pap would be here right now, snapping pics of me?"

I peeked over her shoulder to check. Cassie stood up and searched the crowd, holding her hand over her eyes like a sun visor. "Just because he didn't yet doesn't mean he *won't*, you know."

Mac raised her chin in pure stubbornness. "It's a risk I'm willing to take. I'm so freaking sick of being scared to live. I can't do it anymore. I won't. He might sell me out, but he might not. And I'm willing to take that chance, for the first time in a long time."

I reached out and squeezed her hand. "And if he turns out

to be a jerk, we'll kick his ass for you. Right, Cass?"

"Right." Cassie cleared her throat. "No matter what, we're here for you."

Mac smiled and seemed to relax. The warmth of our friendship flowed over me, and I wondered again how I'd gotten so lucky. They were like my sisters, and I could always count on them. Again, my thoughts flashed to James. What would it be like to have no one in your life you could trust? Talk to? Laugh with?

Mac sniffed. "I know. And I love you."

I decided to break up the serious tone, so I twisted my face and dropped into my best Southern accent. "Now, now. Let's not go getting all mushy and lovey-dovey. This is a vacation. It ain't nothing but fun and games."

Mac laughed. "Please. I don't even talk like that anymore. I stopped when I became famous because my agent didn't want me to be typecast as the little Southern girl."

"Yeah, but it's still fun to do," I said with a grin.

Cassie nodded. "It really is."

We finished eating and discussed where we'd split up for the day. Mac's final words were like a promise and a threat, wrapping me up in a flurry of emotion I couldn't seem to untangle.

"By the time this vacation is over, none of us will be the same. It's going to be legendary. You both just have to make sure you live it to its fullest, like I am. Promise me."

Cassie looked doubtful, but I nodded in agreement. After all, I had gone too far to turn back now.

I kissed them goodbye, reminded them to stay safe, and left to meet James.

CHAPTER
Thirteen

James

I watched her walk toward me. She wore her dark hair loose, the straight shiny strands swishing across her shoulders, and those inky almond eyes peeking at me from behind her bangs. Today, she sported a pair of denim shorts, a simple white T-shirt, and brown leather sandals. No jewelry. Little makeup. And she blew me away more than a Victoria's Secret model shaking her ass on the runway.

Quinn ducked her head as she got closer. I recognized the shyness of the gesture, but in seconds she'd pulled herself to full height and marched the last couple of steps. I loved the dual aspects of her personality, especially her strength, and my body lit up when my arms finally closed around her.

"Hi," she said softly.

I didn't respond. Just bent my head and kissed her slow and deep, reminding her of last night and our connection. I never exhibited such primitive behavior before, but I didn't care. I only knew I needed to mark her and make sure no other guy even sniffed around Quinn this week. She softened beneath my kiss and practically sighed in surrender. I wanted to drag her back on the boat and stay in the cabin, fucking her every way possible until sunset. If we hid away from the world, nothing would ruin this. Nothing would ruin us.

But I promised to show her some actual tourists traps in Key West, and she deserved that.

Slowly, I broke the kiss. Her lips were wet and ripe and inviting. Her tongue slid over her bottom lip as if to catch my taste, and I groaned in agony. A wicked glint lit up her dark eyes.

"Do that again and I'll show you some different types of sightseeing."

A low chuckle vibrated from her throat. "Promise?"

My body locked down to full attention. I playfully grabbed at her but she sprang away, her cheeks red, laughing. "No, no! I want to see Hemingway's house."

"How about I show you his drinking stool and we retire for the day?" I suggested with a leer.

"No. It's beautiful out, and we can't waste it."

"Okay, you win." I grabbed her hand and snugly interlaced her fingers with mine. My spirits lightened and suddenly the day spread out before me in rich promise. "Let's get all the visitor stuff done today so we can relax tomorrow on the boat. What do you want to see?"

She frowned, obviously thinking hard. "Hemingway's house. The southernmost point. Sloppy Joe's Bar. Jimmy Buffett's house. Glass-bottom boating. Sunset sailing. Drink a margarita at Margaritaville. Oh, and the sunset festival on the pier."

My mouth dropped open. "Please tell me you're not serious."

She gave an adorable little pout. "I am. How can I go back home to Chicago and say I've seen nothing?"

"I'm insulted."

She laughed. "Well, it's quite impressive and not nothing, but I can't *tell* people about that!"

"Hmm, good point. Better get started. We have a torturous day of being tourists ahead of us." I tried to tick down the agenda and figure out the best place to start, but she stopped in her tracks and dug her heels into concrete. "What's the matter?"

The playfulness disappeared. Her brown eyes turned serious. "You don't have to babysit me today. I mean, we could always hook up tonight."

Temper reared, but I pushed it back. The idea she thought I looked at her as just a sex toy bothered me. Funny, if she were another woman, I'd dread dragging myself around town when my only purpose was to get her in bed. With Quinn, it was different. I'd go anywhere with her, because her presence made me feel good. But I couldn't dump all that on either of us, so I grabbed her again and kissed her hard enough to make her forget. "I want to be with you." The doubt on her face made me lower my voice and smile. "Besides, I refuse to let you lock me up so you can use me as your sexual slave. I deserve a meal, fresh air, and to be out in public."

She relaxed and laughed with me. And I kept my promise.

I showed her everything. We walked around Hemingway's house with a bunch of other tourists, and enjoyed the lush greenery, open balcony, and numerous cats prowling around the property and peering through bushes. Quinn listened intently to the tour guide, seemingly processing the endless information about Hemingway's hobbies, love interests, and extraordinary writing skills. I'd been there many times before, but this time I saw everything through Quinn's eyes. The architecture and presence of such a powerful legend permeated through the space, making me appreciate things I'd never seen.

We listened to Jimmy Buffett's endless loop of his famous song "Margaritaville," but I learned Quinn was tone deaf and could barely hum the familiar bars without my wincing. She punched my arm and threatened me with her rendition of Adele, so I surrendered and bought her a frozen margarita instead of her usual Sex on the Beach. We feasted on salsa and chips, mozzarella sticks, and fried conch fritters, then moved on to book a reservation for glass-bottom boating.

"Are we going to see lots of fish?" she asked, craning her neck around the plates of glass set up on the bottom of the boat.

"Should be decent. I'll point out some to you when we get started."

I tried not to laugh as she fought off some stranglers who tried to squeeze in her viewing space, until a child wobbled by and gave her a toothy grin. She melted on sight, and ended up helping the baby sit down and cooing at him. She laughed with the mom, and chattered easily. She knew her place in the world at only twenty-one, and radiated an inner light I wished would spill into my own dark soul. But it didn't work that way. My chest tightened with pain, so I excused myself to get a beer and tried to get my shit together.

The boat slowed and the speaker boomed with information on what types of fish they were currently looking at. I sipped my Coors Light, brooding a bit about our differences, and noticed Quinn was holding her stomach.

I put the bottle on the bar and walked over. The baby was banging on the glass, distracting the mother, but one look at Quinn told me what the problem was. She was pure green.

Seasick.

I gently helped her to her feet and she swayed. "James. I don't feel so good."

"Aww, baby, you're seasick. Let's go out on the deck so you can get fresh air."

"I don't get sick," she insisted, but she held tight to my arms and allowed me to lead her out the doors.

"Take deep breaths, slow and easy. Damn, I should've thought of making you take some anti-nausea medicine."

"I don't get sick," she said again, but her voice grew faint, and she moaned.

"Sure, you don't. Probably too busy taking care of everyone else. Let me get you some water. Can you stay here? I'll be right back."

She leaned over the rail. "Not going anywhere."

I hid a grin and got water and a bunch of napkins from the bartender. By the time I got back, she was clenching the rails with a death grip. Her jaw worked as if trying madly to hold back from hurling. "Babe, drink some of this. Look out way in the distance, as far as you can see. And breathe deep."

"Think I'm gonna vomit," she said miserably. "You gotta go."

"I'm not going anywhere. Drink."

She gulped in a breath and took a sip of water. Then creased her brows in a fierce frown as she concentrated on the horizon. I stroked her hair and rubbed her back, waiting it out. Finally, her muscles relaxed. "I feel a little better."

"Good. It should be over soon. I wouldn't advise going back in there. Something about looking at the bottom of the boat as it moves makes a lot of people nauseous."

She drank some more water and leaned into me. My arms slid around her stomach, and I rested my chin on the top of her head. We finished the boat ride in comfortable silence, until the buzzing of my phone interrupted. I fished it out of my back pocket and glanced at the screen.

Adam.

I declined the call and waited to see if he'd text. I hadn't spoken to him or Rich since they promised to stay away from Quinn and me. Probably checking on the stupid bet. I made a mental note to tell them it was officially off, whether or not I'd meet my mentor, but the text threw me off guard.

Dude, confirming party tomorrow at your house. Invited a bunch of new people. Gonna be epic.

Shit. I usually held the parties for spring breakers Sunday, Wednesday, and Friday. They were the big events of the week.

I thought of the empty conversations, alcohol, and half-naked girls who meant nothing to me. Was I ever gonna stop? Why was I even doing it? I was way past the age for spring break. Hell, most guys my age were digging into a career and planning their futures. Disgust boiled in my gut.

"What's the matter?"

Her quiet voice brought me back to the present. "How'd you know?"

"You got all stiff on me. And not in the good way."

I laughed and held her tighter. "Adam texted me about a party I'm supposed to throw tomorrow. If I do it, will you come?"

She shifted her weight and silence settled between us. Uh-oh. "Of course, I'll go." I let out my breath. "I'm just—I'm just not that big into those type of parties." She sounded glum, so I turned her around and forced her to meet my gaze. "I have to tell you something, James."

My heart pounded, but I kept my voice calm. "Go ahead."

"I'm kind of a nerd."

I waited for more, but that seemed to be the big confession. Relief whooshed through my body. "You're a very sexy nerd," I said.

Her lips twisted in a half-smile. "I'm serious. I'm lame. I don't get off on drinking hard, parading myself around, and making endless conversation with people who don't care. I'm sorry. But if you want me to go, I will."

It didn't take me long to make my decision. In fact, the moment I accepted what I was about to do, I was completely at peace. I didn't want to hold these parties anymore. I wanted to spend the day alone with Quinn and let it take us wherever it would. I was done with that part of my life, and it was about time I did something about it.

"I'm canceling the party, Quinn. I've been trying to get out of them for a while now. Hell, I don't even enjoy it. Time for someone else to take over."

She gnawed on her lip. "Don't do it for me."

I smiled and ran a thumb over her now swollen mouth. "I'm doing it for me. Will you spend the day with me alone?"

Her face lit up and my heart stopped. "Yes. And I have a long list of activities for us."

"More?"

Her eyes danced. "Yeah. But tomorrow we'll keep it all horizontal."

The blood whooshed to my other head. "My kind of activities."

"Thought you'd like that." She studied my features, and her hand lifted to push my hair back from my brow. Her gentle touch burned like charcoal against my skin. "You remind me of Gatsby."

"F. Scott Fitzgerald? Didn't they make a bunch of movies about Gatsby? Wealthy guy with a mansion, lusting after a girl from his past?"

She continued her caress, smoothing her fingers down my cheek, across my jaw, and touching the center of my lips. Her sweet scent carried on the ocean breeze and tangled me in its spell. I'd never be able to smell coconut without thinking of her. "Yeah. He has all the money in the world, and holds these lavish parties that everyone flocks to. Handsome, smart, mysterious. He's a celebrity everyone wants a piece of. But inside, he's lonely. Separate from the crowd. He ends up pinning all his hopes on Daisy because she made him feel something."

I felt as if we were on the verge of something huge, and if I said the wrong words, the moment would pass forever. The boat pulled to the dock, and the crew scattered to begin debarking. "Do you feel sorry for Gatsby?" I knew I'd walk away if she said yes. I could take anything but this woman's pity, or becoming one of her pet projects.

She cocked her head. A touch of a smile rested on her bow lips. "Of course not. Gatsby had all the power. Daisy never did." Her dark eyes shimmered with heat and truth and possibility. "He just didn't know it."

A couple bumped into us. I took her hand and led her off the boat, wondering what she meant.

CHAPTER
Fourteen

Quinn

The sunset festival was like a circus with the backdrop of water and sky. I held tight to James' hand as we weaved our way through the staggering crowds and watched performers take turns dazzling us with their talents. Trained dogs doing flips and acrobats were in the right corner; the middle had a man on a unicycle juggling; and the left boasted a woman who seemed to have no muscles or bones, bending her body into insane positions for the approval of strangers.

I munched on popcorn, safely past my seasickness, and the glowing sun began to sink. Music pounded around us— Jimmy Buffett again—and people merged into one group. I enjoyed watching public events for the way separateness merged into unity. Usually, people tried to avoid one another, heads bent to our phones for email, texts, and video games; ears covered by headphones, ducking down to avoid contact.

But today, waiting for sunset, there was magic in the air and everyone sensed it. We laughed and bumped into each other and didn't try to hide.

Excitement built as the three performers melted away and welcomed the sword swallower. He perused the audience, boasting a dangerous tale, and asked the crowd for silence and meditation to avoid injury. His mouth opened and the sword slipped down his throat. I gasped along with everyone else, stunned at the display. I knew James had seen it countless times, but I clung to him in sheer fear that something terrible would happen.

The sword sank in deep, and he slowly pulled it out to the thunderous applause. I jumped up and down and James laughed, his face open and soft as he gazed at me. My heart turned to mush, and my gut churned. I was getting very attached. The fact he'd cancel his big party to spend alone time with me affected my firm position not to feel anything past sex. There was a piece of a lost soul beating within him that called to me. Probably the classic cliché of fixing the wounded, one of my weaknesses. I couldn't walk away from someone who needed me; it was my calling card. But James gave me something priceless, that I've never experienced before.

Magic.

When I was him, I became someone else. Someone better. I was sexy, and confident, and silly, and just me. I'd never felt comfortable enough to shed my outside skin and show a guy my real self. I knew he wasn't faking liking me to get me into bed, we were past that part, but stuck at a crossroads where neither of us really wanted to define what was happening.

"Here's the finale," James pointed out. A tightrope was strung across the dock, over the water, and the performer was climbing the ladder and getting himself settled on the left landing. The sun sank inches lower, hovering on the edge of the horizon. He held a long stick and wore some type of ballet slippers.

The audience fell quiet. He ventured onto the rope, step

after step, making his way to the middle. Filled with poise and grace, his movements flowed into one another as he hit dead center, and the sun dropped out of sight, scattering the skyline with sparks of vibrant orange and blackness.

His shadow was beautiful as he completed his ballet dance over the water, then with a flip, he steadied and reached the right landing.

I whistled and clapped hard until my hands stung. "Do they do this every night?" I asked, craning my head up to look at James.

"Every night," he confirmed. "And it's always crowded."

"Such a beautiful tradition," I murmured. How badly I craved routine in my life. I lived consistently wondering what disaster would await me at home, trying to control things I couldn't. But tradition was sweeter than routine, and brought elements of family, love, or comfort. "I wish we had something like this in Chicago."

He stole some popcorn and fed me first, then himself. "Smaller towns and islands have more unique events like this. Bigger cities are great, but you can get a bit lost."

"Which do you prefer?" I asked curiously.

He paused in the act of chewing. "I'd prefer to settle in a big city and take side trips. I grew up in New York."

"How long did you stay there?"

He shrugged. "Till about ten, I think. Then we moved to Florida. My father runs a big banking empire, so every time there's some type of merger, we follow the trail. We've been in Chicago for a while too, and California."

I tried to be casual, but I was hungry for more information. "Your father didn't try and recruit you for banking?"

A shadow of pain passed over his face. "Yeah, he did. Declared me incompetent for such a career. When I made my first mistake, he pointed it out in a big meeting and humiliated me. Basically told everyone I'd never step into his shoes, but he couldn't reject his son because it was a family business. Then took me in his private office to tell me how worthless I was."

I winced. My dad was a drunk, but I always knew he loved me, even when he screwed up. I couldn't imagine being with parents who were cold. "And your mom?"

"Mom runs charity functions and has little to say in Dad's business. She runs in high society groups, throws big parties, that sort of shit. I tried to be what my father wanted for almost a year, but it was a fucked-up mess, and I finally quit. He insisted I try out some Ivy League careers then, probably by greasing some palms of bigwig assholes, so I flunked out." He shrugged again. "No big deal. They both leave me alone now so I can do what I want."

It sounded good, but realizing your own parents didn't care about you was bound to cause some issues. "What do you want to do now?" I asked.

He stared at me, seemingly surprised by the direct question. A glint of hunger sparked in his ice blue eyes. Oh yeah, he did want to do something. Art? I leaned in, greedy for any information he'd share. Finally, he answered. "More."

So much vibrated within his one-word answer. "Like?" I prodded.

A half-grin tugged at his lips. "Wanna know all my secrets?"

"Yes."

He paused, as if trying to choose his response carefully. "My parents made me feel like a loser for not being what they wanted. I don't even think they meant to do it. They just had an idea of what I'd do, and never cared to see if I disagreed. I was drawn to the artistic field. Painting, drawing, music, acting. Anything that seemed to strip off the surface. I'm so fucking tired of appearances." My heart lurched. He looked so sad, lost, and a tad vulnerable. "I tried taking these classes on sculpture once. Worked my ass off for weeks for a gift for Mom's birthday. It was a takeoff on a *Madonna and Child*, which was supposed to be us. When I gave it to her, she looked so shocked. I thought she'd finally give me a compliment and see what I really wanted to do."

"What did she say?"

His face lost all expression. "Thanked me, of course. She's always polite. Told me the best present in the world would be for me to get a respectable job and stop fooling around with stuff. And that was it. I found it buried in the back of the garage a few days later."

I sucked in my breath. I knew he didn't want my pity, so I did the next best thing. I stood on tiptoe and kissed him, long and deep and gentle. I didn't care about the crowds around us or anything but soothing a bit of that pain he was trying so hard to hide. His arms snagged around my waist and pulled me hard against him, and I lost myself in the kiss until the ground seemed to sway beneath my feet. My breath cut out and I held on hard, desperate to have him fill me between my thighs and take my mouth and swallow me whole. I shook, completely helpless under such raw need, and then he raised his head and stared into my eyes.

"I want you."

My voice broke. "Yes."

"Stay with me tonight, Quinn," he whispered. "Sleep in my bed and let me fuck you for hours, until we don't care about anything anymore."

My blood boiled and I clutched his shoulders. "Yes."

I don't remember how long it took us to get back to his villa. It was different in the silence and the dark, a majestic, multi-level structure hidden in the trees. The pool gleamed an eerie blue, and the endless windows were like eyes peeking out at the world. He led me upstairs without pause, both of us so driven by hunger for each other we didn't need to do any polite routines.

He shut the door behind me. I glanced quickly at my surroundings. His room was a huge suite, with a king-size sleigh bed and majestic food board in dark cherry wood. French doors led out to a balcony, and I glimpsed a huge master bath with a Jacuzzi tub off the open door to the right. The colors were rich brown, dark blue, and creams.

"I want you naked." His blue eyes were so hot they blistered me, roving over my body and probing beneath my clothes. "Take everything off." Oh God, my knees weakened at that sexy, domineering tone. My hands paused on the edge of my T-shirt, but I was trembling so bad I couldn't work the material. He took a step forward. "As much as I'd love a naughty strip show, I can't wait, Quinn. So, let me help you."

His hands covered mine. He helped guide the shirt up over my chest and threw it on the ground. The white lacy bra was simple but pretty, and my nipples hardened under his hungry stare, trying to escape their confines. He cupped my breasts, murmuring beautiful words that lulled me into a trance, and unhooked the front clasp. I arched, and he stroked me, lowering his mouth to tongue my nipples and rub them until I was swollen and tender. In seconds, my denim shorts were gone, along with my lacy bikini bottoms, and I was naked, standing in front of him.

"Fucking gorgeous," he said, his hand already sliding down my belly to touch my pussy. I was wet and ready, as if my body was a robot that turned on a switch set only for him. I panted as my arousal notched higher. He was fully dressed still, and it turned me on. I felt helpless and naked under his control, and I wanted him to do anything and everything to me for his own pleasure.

He seemed to sense my surrender, because he growled a curse and kissed me. Forcing my lips wide, his tongue thrust in and out of my mouth, taking and claiming, the same way his fingers slipped deep inside and teased me to the edge. He bent down and inserted his knee under mine, then lifted. One thigh was draped up and over his, holding my pussy open for his exploration. Never giving me too much pressure, he stroked around my labia, my clit, and inserted three fingers deep, moving back and forth in a rhythm that turned me into a wild animal. I was so wet, I soaked his hand, but he wouldn't let me climax, and the brutal anticipation almost killed me. I bit down on his tongue and twisted, and he gave it to me rougher, shoving me into a pit of sensual depravity that I welcomed. "Come against my hand. Show me how much you need me, how bad you want me. Only me."

"Yes," I moaned, desperate for him, desperate for release. "Only you, James."

His thumb massaged my clit as he thrust his fingers deep in my pussy and bit down on my nipple. The pleasure/pain shocked my system and threw me into orgasm. I clenched around him and cried out, holding on for dear life as my body bucked and shattered with release. I gripped him to keep myself from completely falling apart, and when I opened my eyes, he was watching my face with a fierce satisfaction and possession that almost made me come again. "So hot for me. So wet. I love watching your face when you come. It's the sexiest thing I've ever seen."

"I can't, I can't—"

"We just started." He lowered my leg and smiled, those sinful lips promising me more delights than my body could handle. My legs shook, but he guided me to the bed, and I sat on the edge of the mattress while he removed a few condoms from his pocket and stripped off his clothes. I was past shyness now, and deep into a craving for more from him. When he was finally naked, he stood before me and let me study him. Dear God, he was so gorgeous. Like *David*, an elegant, sensual statue of beauty I wanted to touch and lick and bite. His skin was a deep brown from the sun, covered lightly with hair, and his cock stood straight up—thick, hard, and ridged. My mouth practically watered to taste him. I'd never enjoyed oral sex, but James was different—from his clean, ocean scent, to his spicy taste that danced over my tongue.

He made a move to join me on the bed, but I needed more, needed to know I could make him beg and weep with pleasure the way he did me. I stood up and dropped to my knees. His blue eyes burned and pierced mine. "Quinn."

"Let me," I said. My hands shook as I reached out and touched him. Hot skin stretched over iron muscle, soft and smooth. I fisted his erection from the base and slid all the way to the tip, where a few drops of his come covered his head. "Jesus, Quinn, I may die."

Bolstered by his words and reaction, I grew braver and lowered my head. My tongue darted out to taste and lick like it was a delicious all-day sucker. I learned what parts brought a helpless groan to his lips, learned the way his muscles locked down to stave off his orgasm, learned the dirty words that broke from his lips when I drove him to the edge.

He grabbed my hair and dragged me upward. I rose from my knees, loving his loss of control, and then he was driving his tongue into my mouth and pushing me back onto the bed to spread my knees wide. "I can't wait," he panted, sucking my bottom lip. He fit himself with a condom and slid in with one long, quick thrust.

He owned me in that moment—body, heart, soul. Driving out every thought and emotion I'd ever had under the burning hunger of belonging to him, his cock filled me, his eyes locked on mine, his fingers dug into my hips, and I was his, only his.

"So fucking tight," he gritted out. Sweat beaded his brow, and I wantonly arched up for more, deeper, letting him take and command everything.

"Take me," I begged. "Take me hard."

He did. Over and over he drove his cock into me, rolling his hips to hit my G-spot and cause shimmers of pleasure to spark along my nerve endings. His gorgeous face poised above me, taking in every broken whimper and plea, never slowing his pace until I clenched around him and held on with all my might and gave up.

The climax swept me up, higher and higher, and tossed me into a dark pit where I became only sensation. And still he never slowed, keeping the pleasure coursing through my veins until I rolled into another orgasm until it was too much, and I wondered if I could die from such beautiful agony.

He came and shouted my name. When he slumped beside me on the mattress, I needed his warmth, feeling as if a hole in my soul had been ripped out. Stupid tears blurred my vision, but he sensed my vulnerability and whispered my name, holding me close.

"I don't know what's happening to me," I whispered.

His arms tightened, and I rested my cheek against his chest, our limbs completely intermingled so his body heat seeped into me and I finally stopped shaking. I closed my eyes, overcome by too much emotion, and he lay silent, holding me, for a long, long time.

As I drifted in a fog, I heard his words.

"I don't know either. Just don't leave me."

I fell asleep before I could answer.

CHAPTER

Wednesday
James

What the hell had I done?

I sipped a cup of scalding black coffee and thought about last night. The brew burned my tongue, but I hung on to the brief pain to try and reach sanity. With a few uttered words, I opened myself up for a mess of complications.

Just don't leave me.

The phrase haunted me, way after she fell asleep, until I could only hold her, stare at the ceiling, and wonder how it happened. How did sex get turned around so quickly? I was the master at compartmentalizing physical and emotional demands, but after two lousy days, I was hooked on Quinn Harmon. Her body was like crack, but her smile and intelligence and kindness wrecked my defenses to rubble and left me bleeding. She was everything I dreamed about in a woman, and for these few days, she belonged to me.

Until she left me behind and returned to her life in Chicago.

I took another sip and leaned against the granite island. She'd go back to her real life and forget about me. Maybe share a few stories with her friends, laugh about the great time she had, and concentrate on finding a guy more like herself. Someone with morals, and a real job, and a family. Not a whiny, isolated rich kid who did nothing with his life.

She'd find someone she deserved.

Misery festered like a blister. What did I want out of my life? I hated banking, the law, and medicine. I hated the crap involved in the upper crust society circles I ran with, because I'd never known anything else. Sure, I travelled, but even then I felt as if I was playing at something, trying to show my parents *SEE ME! LOVE ME!* They never did, and I needed to let it go. But if I was going to try and be more, I had to start somewhere.

My fingers itched for a paintbrush or charcoal pencil. Whenever my thoughts skidded out of control, I found my peace in elegant lines, brilliant color, sharp edges. The play of light fascinated me, allowing me to study it for hours and try to reflect it in my work. It was one of the only times I reached peace, allowing another self to surface, one I actually felt proud of.

But what could I do with it? I'd never be good enough for art school. I had no formal training, and all the years of hiding my work from my dad's skeptical opinion and my friends' humoring of my hobby had taken its toll.

I was a pussy. Afraid to go for anything that may be worthwhile. Afraid of...everything.

"Morning."

I jerked and some coffee sloshed over the rim. She stood in the archway, wearing one of my shirts that hung just past her knees. Bare legs and feet, hair messed and tangled, head ducked a bit in a gesture of shyness, my throat closed up and I could only stare. She was so fucking sweet and beautiful. My dick jumped to attention and I fought the urge to drag her onto the table and shove myself between her legs. The other part wanted to pick her up, kiss her tenderly, and protect her forever. I ended up staying put so I didn't freak her out.

"Did I wake you up? I wanted you to sleep in today."

She shook her head and shifted her weight. Those pink toenails jumped out at me. She had such a naughty, dark side mixed with the good girl image I was crazy about. How had the guys ever pegged her a snob or cold fish? "No. I looked for you and you weren't there. And I smelled coffee."

I smiled. "I'll get you a cup. Take a seat." I motioned to the stool and she slid into the high red leather, hooking her feet over the rung. "Milk? Sugar?"

"Just milk, please."

I fixed her coffee and watched her drink it. Her face softened into pleasure, almost the same expression when she began to relax under my touch. I gripped the counter and wondered how every move she made both fascinated me and turned me on. "Good?"

"Yes. I like it strong."

We drank our coffee in companionable silence. I waited for questions about last night, or a long conversation regarding emotions, expectations, or fears, but she never said a word. "Are you hungry?"

She scrunched up her nose. "Can you cook?"

I laughed. "A little. I have a housekeeper for this place 'cause I hate cleaning, but I don't mind fooling around in the kitchen. How about an omelet?"

"Sounds good. Thanks."

I began preparing, grabbing some ham, cheese, milk, and eggs. I couldn't remember the last time I cooked for a woman staying over. It was intimate, and I liked serving her. "Are your friends good with us spending the day together again?"

"Yeah, I'll check in with them later to make sure they're okay, but we kind of planned to be separate for this trip."

"How come? Usually girls flock together and stay that

way."

Uneasiness flickered over her face. I paused in the act of mixing the ingredients and waited for her answer. "Umm, well, Mackenzie proclaimed we all needed to hook up this week, so we weren't allowed to see each other."

I arched my brow. I was half annoyed at her plan to find some guy to sleep with, but hadn't I done the same exact thing? I tried not to laugh as she shoved her face in her mug in an attempt to hide. This was too much fun to pass up. "So I was just part of this master plan to be used?" I asked.

"N-No! I mean, not really, I didn't plan on sleeping with you. I didn't like you!"

"You didn't even like me? Hell, now I really feel used. You just wanted my body."

"No! Crap, you're twisting my words. Besides, you came after me, remember?"

"Forget it. Let me just take off my clothes so you can fuck me. I never thought I could feel so cheap."

"James! I—" She broke off, catching the huge grin threatening to split my face. She gasped and pointed. "You're teasing me! You suck!"

I laughed in delight at the red spots on her cheeks. "Baby, let's just say you can use me anytime you want," I drawled. "In any way, even."

She glowered, those plump lips pursed in a cute pout. "I can't believe I fell for that," she grumbled. "I was afraid to hurt your feelings."

"Using a guy for his body isn't a problem, Quinn," I told her, dropping the mixture into a hot pan.

"I'm not," she said softly. "Are you?"

I spun around. Her serious dark eyes stared back. The question exploded around me, and I realized we'd reached a turning point. Had she heard my plea last night before she fell asleep? Did she know how much she meant to me even after this short period of time? I watched her carefully, wondering what she wanted from me. "Am I *what*?"

She swallowed and lifted her chin in that movement of pure bravery that almost broke my heart. "Using me for my body? Or am I more?"

The sizzle in the pan drifted to my ears, but I stood still, frozen to the spot. What type of answer did she want? The truth? That I was falling in love with my spring break fling and she was going to leave me without another thought? Or was this an opportunity to take a leap and find what I needed to know? If she needed me as much as I did her?

My silence must have been too long, because she forced a laugh and shook her head. "Forget it, I'm so lame. Let's just enjoy what we have and not analyze it. Wow, that smells good."

It would be easy to accept her fake words. Move on without dissecting some scary-ass feelings that could end up breaking both of our hearts. But I couldn't leave her hanging. I wasn't that much of an asshole—not when it came to Quinn.

"You are."

"What?"

I leaned over and pinned her with my gaze. Showing her everything I was feeling and fighting in that brief moment. "I wanted it to be just sex. It would be easier. But you're more, Quinn, much more. Do you understand?"

She quivered, nodding her head. I wanted to go to her, but it was too much, and I had already sacrificed more than I thought I could this morning.

Then she smiled. A beautiful, giving, joyous smile that splintered my reality and left it broken behind me. "I understand."

My heart hurt, so I turned back to the eggs for something to do. I grabbed a plate, slid the omelet on, and served her at the counter. "Eat up. You'll need your energy."

She was still smiling when she took the first bite.

The blare of my phone cut through the air halfway through our breakfast. I got up and checked the screen. Adam. I'd already texted him back to cancel the party, and his continuous texts were getting more and more crazed. Better take it or the guy may show up at my door. "Be right back, I gotta take this," I said.

"Okay."

I walked into the living room and hit the button. "What's up?"

My friend's voice was high-pitched. "What the hell are you doing, man? Are you fucking crazy? We had these parties planned for months—hell, it's a tradition in Key West. You can't cancel on me. I got a ton of people freaking out."

My temper reared, but I kept calm. "Adam, if you want to have a party, you host it. I'm done. I got shit I need to do this week, and I'm not up for hosting more of Girls Gone Wild at my house."

A long groan. "I can't have it at my house! I don't have the space, and it's too damn late to rent a hotel. Hey, I got a great idea. I'll host the party over there. I'll take care of everything, make sure we clean up. What do you say?"

Why did I suddenly feel like I was eighteen again? Rich and Adam were always pushing me to take the lead because my parents didn't give a shit. They were both stuck in their fathers' firms, living the dutiful life I'd always hated, so they looked to me to be the wild one. The one who bucked the system, took no prisoners, and broke all the rules.

I was fucking sick of it.

"No. Just tell everyone it was canceled. There are plenty of bars and booze cruises to do instead. And Friday's party is also canceled."

"Fuck!" Adam's screech echoed, but I didn't care. Time to make myself happy. "Why? Is it that girl you're trying to score with to win our bet?"

I stiffened. I didn't want Adam or Rich to know anything about her. "No. I haven't slept with her yet."

"And you won't. But if you get her drunk at the party, you may have a better shot at getting in her pants. How about that scenario for you?"

I pictured putting a fist through my friend's mouth instead.

"The bet's off. I don't care about meeting Whit Bennigan."

"Sorry, bro, you can't call off a bet midweek just because you're losing. It's still on, and if you don't get us proof, say goodbye to your bike."

I rubbed my forehead. I couldn't think about this shit now, I'd worry about it later. I needed to get Adam off my ass. "The parties are canceled Adam. Tell Rich I'm not changing my mind, and if the bet's still on, leave me the hell alone until Friday."

Silence settled over the line. "Fine. This is fucked up, James. But whatever."

He hung up.

I hit the button. What a mess. I had a bet about Quinn I couldn't stop and a bunch of pissed off friends. Still, I felt good about my decision. I'd figure the rest out, even if I had to lie and give up my bike. Nothing really mattered now except spending as much time with the woman half naked in my kitchen.

I threw my phone on the table and went to her.

CHAPTER
Sixteen

Quinn

I wiggled my toes and relaxed back on the lounge chair. A warm breeze brushed my body, and the sun burned hot on my skin, melting my already limp muscles to wet noodles. The pool glistened in a gorgeous blue that reminded me of James' eyes, and I smiled, shutting out the world, remembering our last heated lovemaking session that blew my mind. We couldn't keep our hands off each other. After breakfast, we spent a few hours in bed, then hit my hotel so I could pack another bag to stay over again tonight. I changed into my red bikini and we relaxed by the pool, until he decided to order some food from the local clam bar and bring it back to the house. I sipped my Sex on the Beach he'd concocted, and enjoyed the absolute decadence of the day. Sex, alcohol, fried food, and rest. I'd reached nirvana.

After about fifteen minutes, I noticed my skin was

beginning to burn again, so I grabbed my drink and went back inside. Maybe I'd explore. I was sure James wouldn't mind, and the house was so gorgeous, I was dying to see the rest of the furnishings and setup. I started on the ground level, peeking into an array of guest rooms, and a sunroom with comfy chairs and bookcases stocked with goodies. I browsed through the shelves, making note of the eclectic collection of art, classic literature, and philosophy, then strolled upstairs. Another bathroom with a spa shower, and what looked to be a media room, filled with high-tech gadgets, a big screen TV, and various speakers. Hmm, maybe we could do a movie night and snuggle up. The idea intrigued me. I kept poking around until I reached the last door at the end of the hall. The knob easily turned under my fingers. I stepped in and caught my breath.

It was more than a room. It was a studio filled with blank canvases, paints, brushes, and different-sized tables. The light poured in from the ceiling-to-floor windows, and the floors were some type of wood, covered with drops of paint in various colors. Fascinated, I walked to the row of paintings and studied the bold lines and colors attacking the white background. It was as if something shimmered beneath, dying to get out, and I narrowed my gaze, trying to look deeper. I wasn't an art major or anything, but had taken a class in college where we went over the basics and famous art. This was unlike any style I'd seen. Who was the artist James collected?

"They're mine."

I spun around and almost spilled my drink. He stood behind me, watching me with a curious expression. His words took a while for me to process. "You did these?"

James nodded. They were mostly portraits, sketched out in bold lines with an array of backgrounds in shocking color. The mingling of charcoal with watercolors was new to me. I flipped through a few more, and began to recognize a pattern emerging. As I made my way through his work, I recognized the development from earlier years to later. There was a growing confidence and better technique. The last one took my breath away.

An old man sat by the dock, his withered hand holding a tattered newspaper, looking out over the water as if a memory had broken his concentration. His face held the lines of one who had loved hard and lost much. The gorgeous symmetry of old and young jumped out at me. Usually, portraits bored me—a line of people I'd never met and didn't know—but James captured an element that made me want to know the subjects. As if I had already met them.

"These are amazing," I said, shaking my head. "They remind me of something that should be in a gallery, not locked up. Have you ever tried to sell any?"

He walked over and stood beside me. "No. Don't think I'm good enough. I never trained."

"Crap, James, can you imagine what you could do with some formal schooling?" My eyes widened when I spotted another small stack of charcoal drawings in a variety of poses. "These too?" I asked.

"Yeah. That's how I started. I was always sketching, doodling. I used to make comics for my friends in school. I spent a lot of time alone in my room, drawing to keep from getting bored."

These sketches were simpler, as if he was building the basics of delving behind the surface of people. He had taken something definable in each of them, whether it was a soft look in their eyes, the clenching of fingers, the tilt of the chin. Each one spoke to me on a different level. I put my drink down on the floor and immersed myself for a while.

When I was finally done, I looked up. "You said you weren't an artist," I said quietly.

He jerked back. "I'm not. I like to draw and paint. I never sold anything. I never trained."

"Why not?"

He let out a breath. "Because it's a hobby. Because it's ridiculous to think you can make a career out of something like this. Everyone has a crafty sort of thing they do in their spare time. Just because I'm rich, I'm not about to force someone to show my stuff."

Bingo. The truth slammed through me. He was born to do this, but had gotten caught up in too many voices telling him he couldn't. Not that I blamed him. After a while, when everyone tells you you'll fail, you begin to believe it. Anger coursed through me at the total waste of his talent and his belief in everyone but himself. "James, you're good. Really good. This is what you're meant to do. No wonder you were strangled at your dad's bank and Ivy League schools. You need to follow this."

"Whatever. Let's go eat."

He turned, but I jumped in front of him. His pretended ignorance was a big fat lie, and I couldn't take it. Not from him. "Don't pull that bullshit with me," I said. "Why can't you admit this is what you want? You have the money to go to art school and study. You have no excuses."

His jaw clenched and his blue eyes sparked. "Exactly! Do you think I want the world believing I bought my way into galleries or school because of my money? I could make a call and get connected with something just from my family name. I don't want anyone's charity, goddammit. I'm not *good* enough."

I practically spit with frustration. "Did you ever even try?" His stubborn expression told me no. "Maybe you'd find out if you submit your work to them and see? Fuck the family name. Just don't use it—make one up and satisfy yourself it's on your terms. You never gave it a shot, because that way you'll be safe. But you're not safe, James, you're just alone. Throwing parties and wasting time and looking for something that's already here. You're a fucking artist! Just be one!"

He fisted his hands and stepped back. I watched the conflicting expressions war for dominance, and suddenly, all that energy hit me like a sucker punch. "It's not that easy."

"It's not that hard."

"I don't know if I'm good! Jesus, don't you get it?"

I got closer to his breaking point, almost scenting his rawness beneath the surface he gave me glimpses of. But I wanted more from him, dammit, I wanted everything he had, whether or not I had the right. "No, explain it to me."

"It doesn't matter."

I let out a strangled cry in pure frustration. "Bullshit! It does matter, it all matters, but you're being a coward by not admitting it. Just fucking tell me what your problem is!"

He gave a vicious curse. He seemed to struggle with temper that was more directed toward himself than with me, but it swirled with a raw emotion that turned me on. This was the James I ached for—his feelings and soul as naked to me as his body. The combination screamed sexual power. "What do you want from me?" he ground out. "Why are you pushing?"

I was breathing hard, aroused, and pissed off at his stubbornness. "What do I want? Oh, that's right. Let me make sure not to demand too much emotion here. Let's just keep it to fucking each other's brains out, okay? Better now?" I knew I was taunting him, but I ached to push past his barriers, and when our bodies connected, all walls came crashing down.

His control teetered, paused, and crashed. "You want to know everything? All the touchy-feely bullshit? Fine—my whole life I had one fucking thing I dreamed of: making it in the art world, on my own. But if I don't have *it*, and I fail, there's nothing left. I shot my load and I got no backup. And won't my fucking parents and friends laugh their asses off? You get it now? You happy?" His voice rose and crashed around me, full of naked and swirling emotions I never glimpsed before.

"Yes, I'm happy now. Now do something about it."

He stared at me, poised on the brink, and then he closed the distance and hauled me into his arms. Blazing blue eyes locked with mine. My nipples hardened and I grew wet.

"Fuck this," he muttered. Slamming his mouth over mine, he kissed me, his tongue thrusting into my mouth and taking what he wanted. I gave it back, pressing myself against him, digging my fingers into his hair and holding on tight. He bent me backward and swallowed me whole, until there was nothing left except what he gave me. My bare thighs scraped his belt buckle, and he ripped off his shorts, shoving down my bikini bottoms, and lowering himself to the floor. Our mouths never broke away, and I whimpered as I grew wetter, wiggling on top of him so I could get his cock deep inside me where he belonged.

He broke away and bit my earlobe. I shuddered. "Condom. Pocket. Put it on."

I fumbled with the wrapper and rolled it on him. He gripped my hips and lifted me over him, my pussy dripping, my nipples begging for his teeth and lips and tongue.

"Ride me, baby. Ride me hard."

I cried out his name as I sank down, taking his cock in one long surge. He buried deep inside me, and I panted for control, digging my nails into his skin as I fought for control. My hair streamed loose over his chest and he groaned, arching up so I was forced to take more. "All of me, Quinn. That's good, so good."

I moved in short spurts, adjusting to his length. Fire shot through my veins and heated me up everywhere. Frantic for more, I moved faster, working my hips, relaxing my muscles, and taking him completely. He controlled my movements for a while, but as I neared climax, I ripped his hands off me and rode him hard and fast and wild, not allowing him any control. He shouted my name and I felt myself coming, the pleasure squeezing me so tight I didn't think I could take a moment more, but I kept coming more and then he followed me, my thighs gripping desperately for balance as every muscle collapsed in ecstasy.

I slumped over, breathing hard, and his hands settled on my ass. It took a while before we calmed down and I felt as if I could finally move. I managed to support myself on my hands and sit back up. He was still inside me.

"I love you," he said.

I should've been shocked. I should've gasped, pulled away,

and tried to decipher what had happened in four days. It was impossible to fall in love with someone so fast, right? I knew that. Yes, I had pushed him, but this confession was way more than I expected. We needed to talk and rationalize what we were doing, and figure out a plan. But nothing mattered anymore. Just the truth.

"I love you too."

I lowered my head and kissed him. Sweet. Tender. My heart swelled in my chest, and I never felt more right about anything in my life. I loved James Hunt.

"Are you ready to eat?"

He'd said the words, but wasn't ready for a long conversation and analysis of our options. Neither was I. I wanted to hold tight to the magic words, be with him, and not think of the future. So, I climbed off him and put out my hand.

James wrapped his fingers in mine and took me downstairs. Things would never be the same between us. And I was glad.

CHAPTER
Seventeen

Thursday
James

*Y*eah. It was official.

I was whipped.

I watched Quinn chatter on the phone with her friend Cassie, going over their arrangements for their flight in case they didn't hook up before. Since I confessed I loved her, we hadn't left the house. We spent hours in bed, trying to top my record of how many orgasms I could wring out of her, and ordered in food so we didn't have to break our rhythm. We swam, napped, and took long walks around the villa, but never ventured out to the bars or beaches or even the boat.

I didn't want to lose any time.

I fixed her a Sex on the Beach and realized our week was almost up. She flew out Saturday afternoon, and neither of us wanted to try to figure out what we were gonna do. She had a year of school left. I was still a walking mess, with no future opportunity or job in sight. Did I really want to follow her off to Chicago like a puppy dog when I had nothing to offer? Would a long-distance relationship work? My mind buzzed with endless thoughts and worries, giving me a headache. I didn't want to ruin a minute of her company, but we needed to have a serious talk. It was the third night in a row I had the same dream about her. We stood by the water, and Quinn reached her hands toward me. A small smile rested on her lips, and sparks of sunlight shot and reflected off the water, blinding me. I wanted to take her hands, but I was never able to lift my arms, and then she disappeared. I called out over and over, but it was too late. She was gone.

I hoped to God it wasn't an omen.

Rich had called me a few times, giving me shit about canceling the parties, and begging me to meet them at the bar tonight. I never answered. I'd be happy staying home with Quinn and trying to make sense of how I could make this work. The idea of losing her made me sick, but I needed to know if she was ready to commit, even if we were apart for a while.

She came out of the kitchen, phone in hand, and smiled at me. Her casual white cotton skirt paired with a hot pink striped tank top gave her a beachy casual look I loved. Especially when I ripped off her clothes and she became anything but. She was a hellcat in bed, giving me everything she had. I'd never known sex could be so intimate and raw and real. It was like I was waking up after years of sleep walking through life. "Cassie and Mac may hit Captain's Cove for a quick drink tonight. Wanna stop in?"

Hmm, the same bar Rich and Adam were going to tonight. "Sure, if you want. What time?"

"We left it loose. I'll check in with them later. Is that for me?"

"Yep." I handed her the drink and she sighed with pleasure. Her skin glowed with sun and hopefully from all the orgasms

I'd given her. Quinn melted the moment I touched her. That type of power invigorated me, made me feel like a God, and I couldn't keep my hands off her. I stroked her arm as she sipped her cocktail. "What do you want to do today?"

She turned her head and cupped my cheek. Her inky dark eyes gleamed with emotion. "I'd love to go out on the boat one last time," she said with a husky hitch to her voice. "Go to the bar for an hour. Then come home. Here."

Home. The word sounded so sweet from her lips, yet so lonely when I thought of her getting on the plane. I pressed a kiss to her knuckles and smiled. "You got it. Finish your drink and we'll go."

We sailed for a few hours while I taught her some basics of boating 101. Her hair whipped around her face and she laughed when she almost got whacked by the sail in an attempt to show off her beginner skills. I kicked her back to the bench so she didn't get hurt, and turned on some music. Her horrible rendition of Lady Gaga was a nightmare, but that was just another thing I adored. A woman who couldn't carry a tune was on my list of go-to traits. She'd never dump me in her quest for *American Idol.*

A brand-new patch of red on her arms made me call out her name. "You're burning again. I have some extra lotion in the closet there." She nodded and poked around in large compartment. "Toward the back," I directed.

She dropped to a squatting position, so I figured the bottle had fallen off the shelf and rolled toward the back. Stretching out, her ass lifted in the air as her hand reached. And then I spotted the perfect lines of a lacy white thong against her skirt.

Oh. Fuck.

I hardened instantly. Jesus, I hadn't seen her in a thong yet. Didn't think she was the type to wear one. Quinn straightened up with the lotion in her hand, no idea that my lust factor had just hit the top of the charts. The cheerful-striped tank only made me feel dirtier knowing what lay beneath the innocent outfit. Quinn in a thong. Kill me now.

I decided to have fun and see if she followed my lead. So far, she liked a few sexy games between us, and I was dying to see if I could push. I marched over to her as she settled on the bench and opened the top of the bottle. She peered up from behind her bangs and frowned. "What's wrong?"

I made my voice sound low and demanding. "What's underneath your skirt?"

Her mouth opened into a little O and a blush of pink touched her cheeks. "Underwear," she said. "Why?"

"You're wearing a thong."

She gasped. "Oh my God, how did you know? Could you see my underwear through the skirt?" I tried not to laugh as she jumped up and twisted around, trying to see if she could spot any lines through the white fabric. She chewed madly on her lower lip. "I hate wearing white, but this seemed like it was thick enough, and I didn't see anything in the mirror, so I figured a thong would be the best thing to wear with white and—I"

"Take it off, Quinn."

She froze. I kept my face firm, gaze trained on hers to see if I was freaking her out or if she liked it. The quick flare of interest and lust told me she enjoyed the hell out of that command. Hmm, interesting.

"Take off *what*?" she asked. Her voice sounded like a weak newborn kitten.

"The thong. Reach under your skirt and take it off." I paused. "Now."

Her breath came quick, and I watched her nipples tighten against her flimsy bra. I was so hard I had a difficult time keeping my sanity, but I was getting used to that state around Quinn. I wondered if she'd obey or laugh it off. I decided to wait her out. I folded my arms, a deep command in my eyes, and holy shit, she gave up a shuddering sigh and began lifting her skirt.

The ground swayed beneath my feet and had nothing to do with the sailboat. I watched the white fabric hitch up above her knees so I got a glimpse of white lace, then she hooked her thumbs on the side and pulled them off. Stepped out of them with grace and held the balled-up panties in her hand.

"Here you go."

I grabbed them. Brought them to my nose and sniffed. Her musky scent ripped through my senses and my sanity. Her pupils dilated so her eyes turned a seething black.

That's when I lost it.

I grabbed her, devouring her mouth like my last meal, and she exploded in my arms in a mass of soft, melty heat. Hands grabbing, nails digging, I pushed up her skirt and dove my fingers into wet heat, curving them the way she liked and hitting her favorite spot. She bucked and moaned, and I eased her to the ground, forcing her on her hands and knees. Quinn panted hard, her ass high in the air, bare to my gaze now that I took away her underwear.

I wasn't going to last.

I ripped open my shorts, sprang free, and covered myself quickly with a condom. Dragging my fingers across her dripping slit, I teased her as I got myself ready, raised myself up, and pushed between her open thighs.

Mine.

Silky wet heat closed around me like a fist. She cried out when I moved, going deep, and I reached around to yank down her tank and play with her breasts. Rubbing her hard nipples, I took her like an animal, and she loved it, bucking and meeting me with every thrust, crying out my name until I felt her shatter around my dick and milk me hard.

"I love you, James! I love you, love you…"

The words sang in my ears and my balls tightened and I came, my body shaking with the force of my release. I pumped until I shot the last drops, turned her around and took her in my arms. She was still shuddering, and I rubbed her back.

"What are we going to do?" she asked, her eyes filling with tears.

I kissed her slow and gentle as I wiped a tear from her

cheek with my thumb. "I love you, baby. We'll work it out. I just found you, and I'll be damned if I'm ever letting you go."

She relaxed in my arms as if we had settled the looming question clouding our happiness. "Okay," she whispered. We snuggled for a while, until we straightened our clothes and I checked on our direction. "I need my underwear," she stated, holding out her hand.

I gave her a wolfish grin. "Hell no. I'm keeping them."

"You can't do that! People will know!"

I laughed. Erotic siren to blushing schoolgirl. Perfect. "Nope. I'll keep it hidden and no one will know." I demonstrated, pushing the lacy fabric deep into my pocket. "When we're at the bar, you'll be thinking of all the bad things I could be doing to you."

She chewed her lip. "Oh my God, I can't."

"You don't have a choice, baby. Now let's get docked and head over to Captain Crow's. The earlier we get there, the earlier I can get you back home where you belong."

I loved the contradictory emotions that skittered across her features. She was completely turned on, but enough of a good girl to be shocked by such behavior. Finally, she seemed to accept she had no choice, but her gaze strayed to my pocket, as if she was nervous. Perfect. She'd be thinking of me all night, even in the bar, and that's exactly what I wanted. My possessive streak ran long and deep when it came to Quinn. The idea of her flirting with anyone other than me made me want to rip off a guy's face. Not very civilized. I'd never experienced such intensity with a woman. She seemed to bring out a bunch of raw emotions I never knew I had, and I was still trying to maneuver through the new shit I was feeling.

As I began to dock the boat and get ready to hit Captain Crow's, I wish I had known the future. If I had, I would've kept sailing and avoided the damn bar at all costs.

Instead, I took her hand, led her off the boat, and hit Duval Street.

Biggest mistake of my life.

CHAPTER

Eighteen

James

The bar was packed. Skimpily-clad bodies grouped together, Jimmy Buffett blasted from the speakers, and groups claimed the large tables with pitchers of alcohol covering every inch of the battered wood. A loud whooping hit my ears, and my crew began chanting my name from the back. Funny, it always seemed flattering before, but now I realized how shallow the shit really was.

"Do you see your friends?" I shouted over the noise.

She shook her head. "Not yet."

"We'll keep a lookout. For now, let me introduce you." She squeezed my hand and I returned the pressure. I figured we'd stay for a drink, Quinn would connect with her friends, and we'd get our asses the hell out of here and back to bed. Where we belonged.

We weaved our way toward the back of the bar, and I

quickly introduced her to Rich and Adam. They gave her a quick once-over, as if they couldn't understand why I was so into her, but finally grinned and made light conversation. The waitress was by my side in a few seconds and Rich ordered a pitcher of tequila, clapping me on the shoulder. "You got this round, right, dude?"

Whatever. I shrugged. "Sure."

"You're the best. Hey, hope you had a better time this week than we did. Things got pretty fucked up since you backed out of our plans."

Adam jumped right in. "Dude, I mean, I respect your decision to cancel—it's your house—but we took a lot of shit. I had a bunch of guys flying in just to crash at your place and party hard. I looked like an asshole."

I shrugged. I was so done with this shit. "Sorry. But I told you, I'm done. Those guys could've flown in and stayed with you."

Quinn interrupted. "Sorry, guys, it was my fault. I wanted to sightsee, so I dragged him around all day."

My heart did a wimpy flip-flop at her attempt to defend me. "Sightseeing, huh?" Rich slurred. "Is that what they're calling it?"

"Shut up, Rich," I warned.

"Sorry." He shook his head. "I'm kinda drunk."

Quinn forced a smile. "No problem. Hey, I see Cassie over there. I'm gonna say hello, be right back." She pressed a kiss to my lips.

"I'll get you a Sex on the Beach," I said.

"Perfect. Thanks."

I watched her walk away and when I turned back, it was like the shit hit the literal fan. Suddenly, I was confronted by a bunch of drunk, revved-up guys who got in my face and began giving me crap.

"Dude, please tell me this thing between you guys is over. Did you do her? Tomorrow's the deadline, you know. Is that why you canceled the party? So you can look good to her?"

I clenched my fists as the anger hit. Adam's lewd comments were getting to me, bad, and it was time to put an end to insulting Quinn. "The bet is off. Take my bike. I couldn't care less. I'm involved with her now."

Rich frowned. "So you did fuck her."

"No." The idea of them tainting our connection by talking about sex made me nuts. Better to get them off the scent. "We never slept together. But I'm into her and hoping for something more permanent."

The guys looked like I had announced I was gay. "You're kidding, right?"

"Fuck off. I'm done with you guys." I made a motion to leave, but they jumped in fast.

"Okay, okay! Fine, we'll back off. We just never heard that from you before, bro. Had no idea you wanted more than a night here and there. You gonna follow her back to her home? Try and be her boyfriend? Get a job and all that shit?"

The words hit my reality barrier and got me nervous. What was I going to do? Jump on a plane and cheerlead her on in her final year of college? Get work in Chicago? Meet her dad? It all swirled together in a burst of images I hadn't really thought out. Or at least, I hadn't wanted to. She had studies and two jobs. A father. Close friends.

I had nothing.

I gritted my teeth and tried to be cool. "We'll work it out."

"Sure, man, sure." Adam and Rich stared at me, their expressions saying I was fooling myself. They knew me well. Knew my background as the mayor of Loserville and playboy extraordinaire. No wonder they were skeptical.

"I'm gonna get Quinn her drink." I reached into my pocket for my wallet and some dude behind me—Jack was it?— bumped into me, laughing hysterically and clutching at my jeans to steady himself.

"James! Sorry, sorry, you buying us another round? You're the man! Here, let me help."

"I got it." I tried to push him away, but he grabbed for my

wallet and a flimsy piece of white lace got torn out with the black leather. I tried to shove it quickly back in my pocket, but Adam spotted it and with a low whistle, tore it out of my hands.

"What's this?" He held up the thong and hooted with laughter. "Holy shit! Nice work, Hunt! Why you denying you scored when you got the proof in hand?"

In slow motion, I watched the events unfold and slide out of my control. "Hey, give them back now."

He threw them to Rich, who cheered and stretched them out. "Nice! I guess you'll be having an appointment with Whit Bennigan after all!"

"I swear to God, if you don't give them back, I'm going to kick your ass," I said coldly. Rage shook through my body. How could I have chosen friends like this? They had no character or motivation for anything better in life.

"Calm down, dude. It's not like your girlfriend is being faithful anyway. She's completely into the bartender."

"What?" His answer distracted me, so I whipped around and found her stretched over the bar. Laughing. The bartender whispered something in her ear that made her blush a bit, and then he slid her a drink. They spoke in an intimate manner, heads close, and she nodded.

The room faded. All I could see was the woman I loved flirting with some tattooed bartender. What the hell was going on? Why would she be putting herself out to a stranger after what we shared? Was this a joke to her? A spring break fling, while she whispered words of love and laughed her ass off on the plane to her girlfriends? *Poor little rich boy, so desperate for affection.* He actually believed they'd have a long-term relationship, and she felt bad enough to jolly him along. At least she got a good fuck out of it. Or two.

All of my weaknesses, insecurities, and fears reared up like a sleeping dragon and roared. Fire hit and spread, burning away the last of my illusions.

I was a pussy. Stupid. So stupid to believe in her.

I turned around. My friends were still talking.

"You won the bet fair and square. God knows she's a cold fish, so you must've warmed her up a bit to hit her next conquest. No worries, James. We got your back. You don't want to get attached to a girl like that."

Ice crystallized my voice. "I'm done with all of you and your sick games. Fuck you."

"Why are you being such a pussy? You nailed her, you won the bet fair and square, and I'm gonna pay up."

"Give me the goddamn panties now," I commanded.

"Now that you satisfied your curiosity, can we move on? We can hold another party Saturday night. It's not too late," Adam called out.

"So it was a bet?"

The room tilted. The rush of noise grew still.

I slowly turned around.

Her husky voice stroked me, like her warm hand sliding over my dick and making me come. Those gorgeous brown eyes flashed with raw pain, but turned cold and hard so fast I thought I had imagined the switch.

I knew I had fucked up.

"Quinn, this isn't what you think."

And as the words spilled from my lips, I knew it was too late.

CHAPTER
Nineteen

Quinn

I left the guys glaring at my back and wondered how much longer we'd have to stay. I couldn't understand how such assholes were James' close friends. He was so much better than that. My thighs brushed against each other and the decadence of not having panties shimmered through me. Who would've thought such things as removing underwear would be so frickin' erotic? I loved how James didn't allow my shyness to hold me back. With him, I became the woman I'd always wanted to be: confident, sexy, smart. Not the practical, nice workaholic who put everybody else first.

I squeezed in by the bar and tapped Cassie's shoulder. She turned and gave me a hug and kiss. "I haven't seen you since Tuesday. You good?"

"Very good. Just wanted to let you know I'm hanging over there with James and his crew."

She narrowed her gaze. "The Ivy Leaguers, huh? They like their beer and tequila."

I laughed. "Yep. Have you seen Mac?"

"Nope, but her hottie is working at the bar."

I looked over and caught tat guy—Austin—slinging drinks and chatting with the customers. "I'm gonna check with him, maybe he knows where she's been. She's not answering her texts."

Cassie frowned. "You think she's in trouble?"

"Nah, she would've called. I think she's up to something and got distracted. Maybe she's writing a song or something. She always loses track of time when she's writing."

"Good thinking. You like him?" Cassie jerked her head toward James.

I smiled. "Yeah. A lot. Tell you later."

"Deal. Just be careful, okay? Remember, no drinks from someone you don't know."

I rolled my eyes. "Cass, I was the one who warned you when we first came on the trip, remember? Besides, we pinky promised. You've been fine, right?"

She hesitated just a moment, her gray eyes flashing with an emotion I couldn't name. "Never better. Go talk to hot guy and get back to yours."

"Thanks." I shifted down to the middle of the bar where I saw an inch of a gap to make my move. Using my elbows, I got close and held up my hand.

Damn. Mac's man was quite good looking, especially with the ink. The fact he could sing was also perfect. I opened my mouth to introduce myself, but he must have recognized me. His eyes lit up and leaned over the bar, ignoring the other patrons. "Quinn, right? Mac's friend?"

"Yes! Austin, right?"

"You got it."

"Listen, I haven't been able to reach Mac. She okay?"

Something flickered over his face, but he nodded. "Yeah. She's been holed up in her room for a bit."

The meaning of that was quite clear. Mac was having fun in more ways than one. Nice. "Got it. Can you just tell her to call me when she's got a chance? I'm not at the hotel—I'm staying somewhere else tonight, so I don't want her to worry if she comes to my door."

His brows drew together. "With that guy?" He motioned toward James and his friends. "I may have to cut them off. Never went through so much tequila in my life, and they get a little over the top when they get together."

Embarrassment shot through me. I hated that Austin assumed James was an idiot. "I think that's a good idea. But don't tell them I confirmed."

He leaned in really far so he could whisper in my ear. "Smart girl. Thanks for the heads-up."

I grinned. He really was a charmer. If I wasn't so gaga over James, I probably would have swooned. "Welcome."

"Listen, Quinn. About Mac."

My heart dropped. "Is she okay?"

He looked uncomfortable, as if debating whether or not to tell me. "There was some trouble. Paps found out about us. She needs you."

I cursed viciously. What the hell? My eyes narrowed. "Was it you?"

He glared right back. "Fuck no. But believe what you want. I don't need this shit."

He turned away, but I grabbed his wrist and stopped him. "I'm sorry. I—I believe you. Is she at the hotel?"

"Yeah. Surrounded by the press. We were on TMZ. Fucking shit."

"Crap. Okay, I'm heading over there now to check on her."

"Why do you believe me?"

I looked into his face and I didn't know. Just a gut instinct. Maybe because it was the easiest thing to believe. Didn't necessarily make it true. "Don't know. Just do."

"Thanks. Wait here." He disappeared for a few moments, then came back with a Sex on the Beach. "Take one for the road. Mac said it's your signature drink."

"Thanks."

He lowered his voice to an intimate pitch. "Thanks for believing me."

Yep. Swoonworthy. I nodded and headed back toward James. I'd need to meet him at the house later maybe, depending on what Mac needed. Poor thing. She deserved to lead a normal life and not deal with this endless bullshit.

James had his back turned toward me and was hissing furiously at his friend. Whoa. He was really pissed, and didn't seem to be fooling around. I tried to capture his words, but the music was too loud, so I got only snatches as I moved closer.

"—won the bet—fair and square—"

"cold fish—must've warmed her up—next conquest—"

"attached to a girl like that—"

"—fuck you—"

Worried, I hurried faster and had just reached the table when a flash of white caught my vision. Adam was waving it over his head, grinning, and Rich and James were going at it, cursing and arguing over something. Why did that thing Adam was holding look so familiar? Delicate, lacy?

Oh. My. God.

My thong.

The true dialogue swarmed around me in a world close to *Alice in Wonderland*.

The blood drained from my body like a husk from a fatal vampire bite. The room swayed under my feet. And at the same time, the inner voice whispered to me that I should've known. Should've known. Should've freaking *known*. It had all been too good to be true.

"So it was about a bet?" I asked.

All the guys turned. Adam lowered my panties and gave them back to James, looking a bit humbled. Rich stared. And James pinned me with his hot blue gaze, piercing past my defenses and touching my core.

But this time, my core was icy. Numb. Better this way, I

told myself. The pain would come later, and that would be a bitch to get through. "Quinn. This isn't what you think."

I tilted my head as if we were having a philosophical conversation. I whipped out my hand and took back my panties, studying them with fake curiosity. "Are we revisiting *Sixteen Candles*? Did you need proof?"

He muttered something vile under his breath and took a step forward. I jumped back. If he touched me, I'd be sick. I needed to get myself through this scene, calm and civilized, so he'd never know how badly he hurt me. He didn't get to know that *ever*.

"You don't get it. Forget the bet. What's going on with the bartender?"

Puzzled, I stared at him. My God, was that what it was about? He made a bet to get me into bed and thought he'd whipped me good to parade me in front of his friends. Was he taking flak from his buddies about me flirting with the bartender? The pieces of the puzzle came together. I felt even sicker. Hands trembling, I put down my drink and drew on every last reserve of strength to get the hell out of this place in one piece.

"Austin?"

He sneered. "So quick to get on a first-name basis. Guess I got taken in by the good girl image. Figured you'd sneak in an extra fling before you go home? Another conquest for you to laugh about with your girls on the plane ride home?"

He didn't even realize I saw him so clearly. He'd fallen for me, but he was too chickenshit to admit it. Much easier to think I'd screw around with other guys than deal with a real relationship. He had no idea what real was. And dear God, he'd made a *bet*...

My voice remained calm. "You'd love that wouldn't you? It would make you feel superior, and ease your guilt about making a bet to get me into bed. What were the terms, by the way?"

"Never mind," he growled.

I directed my attention to Rich and Adam. "Tell me the truth. For God's sakes, the jig is up. Might as well spill."

Rich was drunk enough to listen to me. "Get you into bed by the end of the week. If he lost, we got his motorcycle."

Humiliation slithered like snakes in my gut. "And if he won?"

Rich cleared his throat. "We hook him up with Whit Bennigan as his mentor. He's a famous artist."

I'd heard the name and knew he was making a huge reputation in the art world. I forced a smile. "Well, good, at least you got something respectable out of it. I do wish you luck with your art career. I better go and leave you all to celebrate."

James grabbed my arm. His touch sizzled, but I bared my teeth, not able to handle the contact. "Don't. I was never gonna go through with it."

I tried to control my shaking. "Oh, I get it. You never actually said the words to your buddies, 'yes, it's a bet.' Did you?" Silence. "Did you say it, James? Tell me."

"I-I-I. Fuck. I said it, but I didn't mean it."

My blood ran cold. "Got it. Thanks for the clarification. Now let go of me." He dropped his hand and looked frantic, pushing his hands through his hair.

"Please, Quinn, it's not what you think. The bet. I never went through with it. Who's Austin?"

Oh no. It wasn't going to be that easy for him. I smiled. "A friend. He's cutting off your tequila, by the way, so you may need to find another party place."

Adam waved his hand in the air and began laughing. "Let her go, James. She's probably like her famous friend, Mackenzie Forbes. Puts on a good act, but screws everyone behind the scenes."

The second jolt of horror punched me back. "What are you talking about? How do you know about her?" The betrayal was too much. The bet was bad enough, but breaking my trust was beyond forgiveness.

Adam laughed harder. "Did you really think you could

hide America's Sweetheart? She's a country music star. At least I got some money out of it."

I shook with fury. "What are you talking about?" I whispered. "Oh my God. Was it you? You sicced the reporters on her?"

"Just one. Got a good payoff though."

James grabbed him by his shirt collar and shook him hard. "What the fuck did you do, Adam?"

"Get off me, dude. You're nuts!" He stumbled back. "I'll put you in the cut of money if you want. Damn, you're so fucking touchy lately."

James met my gaze. His eyes pleaded for me to understand. "I never told them, Quinn," he stated. "I swear to God."

It was too much. Too many lies to take. I needed to escape before I burst into tears. "It doesn't matter anymore. I'm outta here."

"Quinn—"

"Don't follow me, James. I mean it."

I turned and pushed my way past the crowds. I stumbled out on Duval Street, but I'd only taken a few steps before someone grabbed by arm. I yanked away, trying to beat James off me, but the sound of Cassie's voice broke through.

"Sweetie, it's me. What happened? Oh God, are you okay?"

A sob caught in my throat, and suddenly, I was in my friend's arms for a comforting hug. "He made a bet, Cass. A bet to get me into bed, and I had no idea. I thought I'd fallen for him."

A blistering array of curse words rose up to my ears. Cassie squeezed me tight. "I'll kill him. Wait here and I'll be right back."

A broken laugh escaped and I hung on to her. "No, he's not worth it. Oh God, I'm a mess. And there's more. His stupid friend blabbed about Mac to the press. The paparazzi are swarming her right now—Austin tipped me off. Mac probably thinks he did it, but it was James. Did you know about this?"

Cassie pulled back and gasped. "This is a mess. No, I

haven't heard anything yet. What should we do?"

I sniffed and tried to get my head on straight. My heart was already in tiny pieces, but I needed to concentrate on my friend. "Listen, I'm going up to her room. Austin said she was holed up."

Cassie looked worried and glanced back at the bar like there was something important going on. Or someone. "Want me to come with you?"

"No, stay. I don't think Mac needs both of swooping in if she's trying to lay low. And I need some time to process."

She looked torn, and shifted from foot to foot. "I don't know. I hate leaving both of you alone when all this stuff is going on."

I squeezed her hands. "Cassie, go back to the bar. For God's sakes, one of us has to have a good wrap-up to this week. I'll check in with Mac and we'll be fine. Text us later."

"Sure?"

"Sure."

We hugged briefly. I made her promise not to kill James or his friends, and I headed back to the hotel to find out what the hell was going on. When I saw the news trucks and the crowds clogging the hotel, my heart sank. Too late. Poor Mac was probably trapped inside and couldn't get back out. I had to show my key to the lobby, and then make my way past her bodyguard, who let me right through.

Mac's eyes widened when she saw me. I probably looked like a mess. "Are you okay?"

I nodded. "Yeah. I think. What the hell is going on, sweetie? Why didn't you tell me about getting busted by the pap?"

She dragged me into the room. "I couldn't deal. I wanted you to have a nice vacation and not worry about me."

I dragged in a breath and just blurted out the truth. "Austin didn't leak the news."

"I know. I mean, I thought he did at first, but then I realized I was wrong. But it was too late." Mac blinked back tears. "How did you know about it?"

I lifted my chin. "It was me."

She laughed. "Really funny."

"I'm not kidding. I didn't actually do it, but I might as well have." I collapsed on the couch and covered my face with my hands. "I told James about you. Told him I was here with you. I trusted him, and his friend…he did it."

Mac sat down beside me and rubbed my back. "James told them?"

"No. James' buddy. Dickhead Adam." I uncovered my face. "He must have been eavesdropping…or maybe James told him. I don't even know."

"It's okay. That's not your fault."

I shook her head. "But it is. I told James. If I hadn't told him, then you'd—"

"I'd still be me, and chances are? Someone else would have figured it out," she stated. "It was only a matter of time, really."

"Mac…" I hugged her close and kissed her cheek. "Thanks for not being pissed. You're too good to me."

"Please. I'm not good enough." She released me. "You didn't do anything to be ashamed of. All you did was trust a boy…"

"And look where that got me."

"All three of us made a mess of things down here, didn't we? What happened to carefree sex and fun? Wasn't that what I ordered us all to find?"

"I don't know." I shrugged and tried not to think of James. Of how bad I still wanted him. Of how stupid I felt to trust him. "Maybe the two don't go hand in hand."

She got up and cracked open a bottle of wine. "I think we need this, and you're going to tell me everything as we get drunk together and talk about how much boys suck. Deal?"

I let out a half laugh. "I think I can agree to that. Let me text Cassie and let her know we're okay. I ran out on her, told her about the press, and left her alone. Someone has to save this vacation."

"Good thinking."

We spent the next hour drinking wine and confessing our escapades from the past few days. I cried on her shoulder, she returned the favor, and when I finally crawled back to my own room, I felt a bit better. I was still torn between wanting to die and wanting to kill him, so I decided to do the only thing left where I didn't have to think.

I curled underneath the blankets, still dressed, and fell asleep.

CHAPTER
Twenty

James

She fucking left me.

I stared at the closed door. The room swayed like I was a polluted drunk, but I didn't move. Rich slapped me on the back and told me it was better this way. Adam apologized for springing the Mac thing on me, then offered me some of the money. Rich said he'd set up the appointment with Whit Bennigan.

I was in a fog for a while. Just sat there, going over the incident in my head, knowing I fucked up, but not knowing how to fix it. Every way I looked at it, I felt completely beneath her, not worthy to be the one she loved. But to let her go, believing she was nothing to me? I couldn't let her go like this.

My attention drifted toward Cassie, who stared at me with such hate I figured she'd like to rip my dick off for fun. She'd run out after Quinn, but now she was back. Why? Because

Quinn laughed off the whole thing and didn't need her?

I was so fucked up. The moment she found out about the bet, I should've dropped to my knees and begged her to let me explain. Especially about the thong.

But no. All I could think of was the asshat bartender who probably deserved her more than I did. I got so jealous I went apeshit, and now I may have lost her for good. Quinn wouldn't fuck with a guy's head for fun. Then Adam had to go and make her believe I betrayed her.

Jesus, this was like a psycho TV show that was way worse than *The Walking* Fucking *Dead*.

I needed to get my shit together and find her. Make her understand that I was sorry, that I wouldn't hurt her, that I'd do anything to make it up to her. Force her to understand I'd never betray her trust and I wasn't the one to tell Adam about Mackenzie.

I walked away while the guys called out my name and begged me to return. When the door shut behind me, I knew it was symbolic. I was done. No matter what happened between Quinn and me, there'd be no more parties, or villas in Key West, or fake friends who didn't even know who I was. I needed to start over and find a life for myself that was real.

I knew she'd be at the hotel. It didn't take me long to walk there, but even though I had her name and room number, they wouldn't let me into the building without a keycard. The news reporters were jacked up for a sniff of Mac, and it was a shitstorm. After a good forty minutes of staking out the hotel, I did what I do best: took one of the back doors, pressed a crapload of money into the hotel guard's hands, and got through. The stairwell took me to her floor, and I thanked God I didn't have to try to get to the penthouse, which would be *Mission* Fucking *Impossible*.

I knocked on Quinn's door. I figured she may not answer, but I'd wait outside her door until she had to leave.

"Quinn." I knocked firmly. "It's me. Please open up. I need to talk to you."

The silence rolled on.

"Quinn. You deserve to know the whole truth before you get on that damn plane. I'll answer all your questions. Please."

Silence.

"I'm staying out here all night if I have to. I'll follow you to the airport, and won't leave your side until you give me a few minutes. Please."

The door swung open.

I stepped into the room and my heart lurched. Her beautiful eyes were swollen and red from crying. Tendrils of hair stuck to her cheeks, and her clothes were wrinkled, like she'd just gotten out of bed. A tight burning squeezed my chest until I felt close to tears myself.

"I'm so sorry, baby," I whispered. "I fucked up. I never meant to hurt you."

"I know." She shuddered and walked to the side table to grab a bottle of water. She took a few sips and finally met my gaze. "Tell me about the bet."

I stood before her, ashamed, and told her the whole truth. "I was knocked out when I first saw you. Sexually attracted and intrigued. The guys were acting stupid, saying it would be impossible to get you into bed, and offered me a bet. Get you into bed by Friday and get proof. I agreed, but you have to believe me, Quinn, I cared nothing about the bet. The moment I talked to you, the wager went out of my head. It was always about you and getting close to you. Midweek, the guys called and asked me, and I told them the bet was off."

"Did you tell them we slept together?" she asked. Her hands wrapped around her stomach like she was trying to support herself. All I wanted was to take her into my arms and comfort her, but I didn't move. She'd probably give me a right hook if I tried to touch her right now—and I deserved it.

"No. I told them we never slept together, because I couldn't handle the crudity. Trying to make it about sex when it was more. So much more."

She pondered my words, staring back at me. Hope leaped.

She believed me. I could tell in her eyes, she was disappointed but on the verge of accepting my confession as truth. "What about my underwear?"

I winced. What a nightmare. "That had nothing to do with it. I was getting my wallet out, and one of the guys grabbed for it, and your thong slipped out of my pocket. Stupid mistake. Before I knew it, Adam grabbed it and began waving it around."

"And the paparazzi? Did you tell Adam?"

"No. I'd never tell your secrets. I never even mentioned Mac to Adam. He must've seen her around the island and made the move himself. Do you believe me?"

She spoke very softly. "Yes."

Hope pounded through me. "I'll do anything you want, Quinn. I just want you to forgive me."

I held my breath. Finally, a sad smile crossed her face. "I do, James. I forgive you."

I ached to close the distance between us but something else was wrong. She didn't seem happy, and suddenly, tears filled her eyes. "Baby, please don't cry. What can I do?"

I moved toward her, but she jumped back again, and shook her head hard.

"No, don't come near me. I have to get this out. The bet was stupid and juvenile, but I believe it didn't mean anything to you. But this is much more than that. What about Austin?"

I jerked back. "What about him? I admit, I lost it. Got jealous. Are you going to tell me who he is?"

"He's Mac's guy. Only saw him a few times, but I was trying to get a hold of her, so I left him a message to take to her. He warned me about the reporters, so that's why we were talking." I relaxed. Thank God. I was right; she'd never betray me. "But you didn't believe me, did you? You let your friends humiliate me in that bar without saying a word. You got cold and accused me of trying to have more fun."

Shame flowed through me. Fuck. What a mess. "I don't know what happened. I freaked, but I would've calmed down eventually. I just needed time to work it through."

"It's more than that, James." Her voice broke. "Don't you understand? You don't believe in us. How can you, when you can't even believe in you?"

"That's ridiculous, of course I believe in us."

"No. You're lost. You deny you're an artist, surround yourself with people who don't know who you really are, and go through life thinking it's enough. You'd always be worrying if I was about to go on to the next big thing. You don't *trust* me. Maybe because we didn't get enough time."

"Don't say that. I got deeper into you than I ever imagined I could, and it's more than your body." Frustration roiled in my gut. I paced the hotel room, needing something to do. "I trust you. You're putting ideas and words in my mouth. I want to try this—try a real committed relationship with you."

"You're not ready." She lifted her chin, and the tears disappeared. All I saw was a distant, faded image of the woman I loved; the woman who screamed in my arms as I pounded into her; the woman who looked at me with her heart in her eyes. "You need to make some decisions with your life and figure out what you want. You can't do that with me at your side."

The knowledge she was slipping away from me right before my eyes made me crazed. With three long strides, I grabbed her shoulders and leaned over. The heat was still there simmering, the sexual energy an immediate flare, and her eyes darkened in response to my touch. "Am I not good enough for you?" I ground out. "Is this what it's about? You don't want me hanging around Chicago, messing up your chances to find someone who's worthy?"

Her face softened, and I knew I'd lost. "No," she whispered. "But you don't believe you're good enough for me. I can't fight that. This isn't going to work, James."

"It will. We'll make it fucking work."

I slammed my mouth over hers. My tongue thrust between her lush lips, and I drank her deep and hard, bending her over so I could ravage and plummet every inch of her mouth. She moaned under the assault, and hung on, responding so sweetly and completely I softened the kiss and let the sensations rock through me. I stopped trying to control the kiss, and just let myself feel. And it hurt.

She tasted fruity from the cocktails, and her skin heated beneath me. I smelled her arousal, and knew I could easily slip my fingers under her skirt and bring her to orgasm with a few strokes. Then she'd forget. I could make her forget. "You need to go," she managed to get out between kisses. "Let go of me and leave."

I released her and stumbled back, breathing hard. "Don't do this," I ground out. "*Please*."

She crossed her arms in front of her chest and tried to hide her shaking. "I have to. I'm going home Saturday. Figure out what you want. Who you are. I can't do it for you."

My heart twisted. "You're leaving me?"

She chewed her lower lip. "I have to."

I almost sank to my knees to beg her to stay. I'd do anything. But then I realized it was too late. In some distant part of my brain, I also realized she was right.

I had nothing to offer. I didn't know what I was doing.

I needed to let her go.

"I love you, Quinn."

With my words echoing in the air, I left the hotel room.

CHAPTER
Twenty-One

Friday
Quinn

I'd lost him.

I stayed in my hotel room most of the day by myself. Cassie and Mac both stopped in to babysit me for a bit, but I shooed them away, wanting to be alone.

I stayed out by the balcony, wrapped my arms around my knees, and stared at the rollicking pool scene for hours. I ordered room service, packed, and got ready for the return trip. My phone remained silent. No message from James. No more knocking on my door.

He was gone, just like I had requested.

It was for the best, but my heart and soul didn't give a crap. I felt broken. How could five lousy days completely change my life? How would I ever get over him?

Day turned into night. Night turned into morning.

I got ready to get on the plane and go home.

James

I'd lost her.

I stared at the empty bottles of liquor lining the tiki bar. I was already past drunk, but I needed desperately to pass out so I could sleep. Her face haunted me. The sound of her voice whispering my name burned my ears. The scent of her sweet, hot pussy tortured my sanity.

I thought about trying one more time, but already knew it was over. She needed a man who was whole, and I'd already proved I was a ghost. Would I ever figure it out? Would I finally have enough guts to get my shit together?

I didn't know. Just realized I was broken without her.

Day turned into night. I drank.

Finally I passed out.

My last image was Quinn standing by the lake, a sad expression on her face as I frantically reached out for her. But it was too late. She turned and disappeared into the sparkling sunlight while I watched her go.

Epilogue

Six Weeks Later
Quinn

"Okay, class dismissed. See you all Monday."

I sighed with relief, closed my books, and began packing up for the weekend. Of course, I had two extra shifts at the Senior Care Home, and an intense session for the rehabilitation clinic, but I didn't care. I hadn't been sleeping well, and Mac and Cassie had been giving me crap about decreasing my workload, but I ignored them.

It kept me busy. It kept me from remembering.

I stared out the window and studied the campus grounds. The temperature had dropped this week and hovered in the low fifties. I missed Key West. Sometimes, it felt like a magical dream. The sun and sand. The decadence of the numerous Sex and the Beach drinks. And James. The endless, sweet ecstasy of being held by him, shuddering into orgasm after orgasm.

Shaking my head firmly, I threw the books in my backpack

and headed out. I missed him every day. For the first week, every time my phone rang or beeped, I'd jump, my heart crazily beating as I checked the screen and prayed it would be him. It never was. After a full month passed hearing nothing, I knew he'd moved on. Without me.

I tightened my coat from the chill of the wind and trudged across the main square of the campus. What had I expected? I'd told him clearly to get his shit together and that we wouldn't work. Most guys couldn't handle such truth, and he probably thought it was the biggest rejection of his life. And it was. But I still loved him. Maybe I'd always love him. I pictured myself ten years from now, studying the paper and finding an article showcasing the new hot artist, James Hunt. He'd be married and happy, long forgetting me, and I'd be single with lots of cats.

Ah, hell. Get over it, Quinn. It was a brief fling and he'd moved on. Maybe he loved me for those few days, but wasn't that cliché famous for a reason?

Out of sight, out of mind, dude, I said to myself. *He's so over you.*

"I prefer absence makes the heart grow fonder," a voice drawled. "Still talking to yourself, huh?"

I whipped around. My backpack dropped to my feet. I gasped.

James stood before me. He was gorgeous. Dressed in worn, tight jeans, with a leather bomber jacket, his dark curls blew in the wind and fell across his arched brow. Those full lips quirked upward in the corner, giving him a bad boy look that had my breasts tingling and my core wet in seconds. Oh God. If he got near and touched me, I'd die. Even a few feet away, I caught his scent, the gorgeous spicy, musky smell that woke up all my senses.

"Wh-What are you doing here?" I couldn't stop staring and eating him up with my gaze. He seemed to have the same problem. Those piercing blue eyes met and held mine in its grip, probing and testing my barriers.

147

His half-smile disappeared. "I moved here."

I almost swayed on my feet, dizzy with need and hope. My palms dampened. "Why?" I whispered.

He shrugged. "Because I love you. Because you were right. I didn't know who I was. I'm still working on it, but I have a plan. I sold the villa in Key West and bought a small studio instead. No more parties, just me and my boat and a good sunset."

My lower lip trembled. "Sounds perfect."

He smiled. "Yeah, it is. I spent some time alone, and decided what I want out of my life. I came up with two main things."

Fear hit me as hard as hope did. The question hovered on my lips, but I was so screwed up, I just kept staring at him, hoping he didn't disappear. *Please say me*, my inner voice begged. *Please tell me you figured it out so I don't have to let you go again.* Finally, I spit out the words before I jumped him. "What are they?"

"Art. I enrolled in an art school and got in on my portfolio, not my family name. I got a job in a studio helping kids learn expression through drawing and painting. I rented a workspace in town, my own loft apartment, and now I'm settling in."

Holy crap, he wasn't kidding about figuring out what he wanted. He had it together—and he hadn't mentioned me once. My breath came in sharp gasps, and I battled the need to kneel over and suck air from a paper bag. So lame. The love of my life came back and I was on the verge of a panic attack. "Sounds like you've got it all. What else could you possibly need?" I managed to ask.

His smile came back, sweet and full of emotion, and vulnerability. "You, Quinn. I need *you* in my life, in whatever capacity you're comfortable with. As my lover, my girlfriend, my friend. I'll take anything I can get. I want time to prove to you who I am, and how we are together when you're with the real me. The one only *you* saw in me."

I swayed on my feet. The man I had fallen in love with was

already extraordinary, full of passion, ideals, and tenderness. But the man in front of me today was even stronger—in his confidence and belief in himself. And us.

He was everything I ever wanted.

"Yes."

He stared at me. "What? Just....yes? I don't want to freak you out by moving here and bursting into your life and—"

I rushed into his arms and tackled him. He fell back on the ground, and I kissed him, crawling all over him while he laughed and kissed me back and held me tight. "Yes," I said again. "Yes, yes, yes."

His arms tightened around me. I didn't want him to ever let go. "Ah, Christ, I love you. I fucking love you, Quinn, and nearly went out of my mind after you left. But it was worth it. This time, I'm not letting you go. Ever."

"Good. I love you too, James Hunt."

We rolled around on the grounds of the campus, kissing and giggling and embracing the future. It may be unknown, and we had a long road to travel, but there was hope, and finally we were together.

The End

Want More Sex on the Beach?

BEFORE YOU
By Jenna Bennett

It's all fun and games

I had a simple plan for spring break.

Sun, sand, and a hot guy. Sex on the beach with no strings attached.

A chance to get rid of this pesky virginity once and for all.

And when I met Tyler McKenna, I thought I had it made.

Until someone gets hurt

But then girls started turning up at Key West landmarks. Girls who looked like me, but with one crucial difference: They'd all been drugged and relieved of their virginity.

The virginity I still have. The virginity Ty refuses to take.

And now I've begun to wonder whether there isn't more to him than meets the eye.

Suddenly, sex on the beach doesn't sound so good anymore...

BETWEEN US
By Jen McLaughlin

I'm just a girl...

I'm a famous country star who's spent her life cultivating a good girl persona to avoid bad press, but I've reached my limit. I'm going away for spring break with my two best friends from college, and we've vowed to spend the vacation seeking out fun in the sun—along with some hot, no-strings-attached sex. The only thing I needed was the perfect guy, and then I met Austin Murphy. He might be totally wrong for me, but the tattooed bad boy is hard to resist. When I'm in his arms, everything just feels *right*.

And I'm just a guy...

I'm just a bartender who lives in Key West, stuck in an endless cycle of boredom. But then Mackenzie Forbes, America's Sweetheart herself, comes up to me and looks at me with those bright green eyes...and everything changes. She acts like she's just a normal girl and I'm just a normal guy, but that couldn't be further from the truth. My past isn't pretty, you know. I did what I had to do to survive, and she'd run if she learned the truth about my darkness. But with her, I'm finally realizing what it's like to be *alive*. To laugh, live, and be happy.

All good things must come to an end...

About the Author

Jennifer Probst wrote her first book at twelve years old. She bound it in a folder, read it to her classmates, and hasn't stopped writing since. She took a short hiatus to get married, get pregnant, buy a house, get pregnant again, pursue a master's in English Literature, and rescue two shelter dogs. Now she is writing again.

She makes her home in Upstate New York with the whole crew. Her sons keep her active, stressed, joyous, and sad her house will never be truly clean.

She is the New York Times, USA Today, and Wall Street Journal bestselling author of sexy and erotic contemporary romance. She was thrilled her book, The Marriage Bargain, was ranked #6 on Amazon's Best Books for 2012. She loves hearing from readers and is very interactive in social media. Talk to her on Twitter, Facebook, or email. Visit her website for updates on new releases and her street team at www.jenniferprobst.com.

Other Books By Jennifer Probst

The Bestselling Marriage to a Billionaire Series
The Marriage Bargain
The Marriage Trap
The Marriage Mistake
The Marriage Merger
The Book of Spells

The Searching For Series
Searching for Someday
Searching for Perfect

Executive Seduction

All The Way

A Life Worth Living

The Steele Brother Series
Catch Me
Play Me
Dare Me

This paperback interior was designed and formatted by

www.emtippettsbookdesigns.blogspot.com

Artisan interiors for discerning authors and publishers.

Made in the USA
San Bernardino, CA
08 April 2014